HUM...

A NOVEL

KYLE CORNELL

To my Pomeranian children Mia and Charli

"A good friend will always stab you in the front."

—OSCAR WILDE

PROLOGUE

The man gasped and sat up. His vision was blurry, but he could tell that he was sitting in the middle of a street. Loud screams erupted in the distance. Pressure suddenly built in his chest, so he doubled over and released a phlegmy, barking cough. Plumes of sparkling blue smoke poured out of his mouth and slithered into the air. *What the hell is happening?* he wondered.

As his surroundings came into focus, he looked down and his heart almost stopped – his right hand, drenched in thick, red blood, was gripping a sharp dagger. His eyes followed a trail of blood that led away from him and they eventually landed on the body of a gray-haired woman who was lying in a pool of blood.

"M-Mom?" he choked out. He threw the dagger down and dragged his body over towards her.

"Who...Who did this to you, Mom?" He pressed his hands to her stomach, but her injury was too severe; a steady river of blood continued to pour out of the entry wound.

"Wh...What did you do?" she gasped. Her eyes bulged wildly in panic.

"I-I don't know! I don't remember! Please, Mom, don't leave me." He sat down next to her and cradled her head in his lap. Tears poured down his cheeks.

"What did...you..." She gurgled and, with one last gasp, her eyes rolled up into the back of her head and she died.

A wave of anger and despair washed over him, causing his mind to shatter into pieces, and he threw his head back and released a howl of pain that tore through the night.

CHAPTER ONE

A high-pitched whistle reverberated throughout a vast, multicolored wormhole. It cut through the swirling, pastel-shaded air like a dagger. Moving through this wormhole was the source of the noise, a serpentine, porcelain-white locomotive that sped along on floating railroad tracks that crackled with energy. Inside the train, a young man named Cole Bennett nervously flipped through the pages of a glossy aviation magazine while seated in the cushy front compartment. The name of this flying locomotive was *The Astrolabe.*

He was startled by a soft *thump* that filled the quiet compartment -- something large and heavy had struck the side of the train. Cole put the magazine down, stood up and stretched, and strode over to a square window. He pushed aside the lace curtains to reveal a jumbled assortment of vintage items floating by in the air: a large poster of Ronald

Reagan spun and twirled slowly; two flashing arcade game systems bumped into each other and popped with the sounds of Donkey Kong; a silver Delorean revved its engine and drove by.

"It looks like we're getting close. Now, I'm going to ask again, Dad..." Cole's eyes shifted to the armed security guard that was standing silently in a corner of the compartment. His stern face held no emotion. "You're *sure* that President Carver isn't going to find out that we're using *The Astrolabe* again, right? We agreed that we wouldn't use it for personal matters. Remember?"

An older man with a thick grey moustache and thinning hair looked up from the notebook that he was scribbling in. Cole's father, Arthur Bennett, put his pen down and smiled.

"Of course, son! I always make sure that everything is in order before setting up something like this. Besides, we've done this before. Remember? I took you, Gabe, and Brody to watch the construction of the Great Pyramid of Giza?"

Cole's mind abruptly filled with images of coarse, yellow sand and stone pyramids soaring into the sky.

"And Sergeant D'Nozo is *very* discrete. Which reminds me..." He pulled a thick wad of bills out of his pocket and put them in the security guard's hand. "Besides, at the end of the day, this is *my* train. We'll be fine. Isn't that right, Mr. Montgomery?"

"Absolutely s-s-sir!" the train conductor replied, smiling cheerfully. He stood at the front of the train compartment operating *The Astrolabe's* main control panel, its many levers and buttons glowing brightly. He was a mechanical, or a mechanized human being, and his entire body was constructed out of sheets of silver and bronze pieces. Cole wanted to continue arguing, but he knew it was pointless. He bit his tongue and changed the subject. "Anyway...we're looking for a clue to a password, right? Which will unlock some kind of airship model?"

"Not just *any* airship model, Cole -- the F-78 blimp fighter model that my father and I built together years ago! Supercruise settings, mini heat-seeking missiles, and realistic mock 5-6T engines. A beautiful piece of machinery. Pop assumed that I would always remember the password to the safe, but...I'm ashamed to admit...all these years later and I just can't remember it. And since he died while I was away, I never got the chance to ask him again. That airship means a lot to me."

"W-W-We've a-a-arrived!" Mr. Montgomery announced. He stepped on the brake, and, with a low groaning sound, *The Astrolabe* slowed down and slid to a halt in front of a white Decade Station. A glossy white metal awning arched over the station and cast a long shadow over the white, wooden floorboards.

"Alright D'Nozo, guard the Decade Station. We'll be back in about two hours," Arthur said. The security guard nodded but remained silent. Arthur waved goodbye to the silver mechanical conductor and then exited the train, Cole following closely behind him.

"Do you think we'll find the clue sooner than that? I can't be late to class," Cole said. He looked down at his wristwatch anxiously.

"Well, son, I told you that you didn't need to come with me," Arthur replied. He stood in front of a clear and cylindrical podium that was positioned at the center of the Decade Station and tapped the glass screen on the top. It awakened and glowed softly.

"Dad, I'm not going to let you do this by yourself! What if something happened to you again?" Cole replied testily. In all fairness, his fears weren't completely unfounded: two years before, Cole and his friends were forced to embark on a long and perilous journey through time, all the way to the Mesozoic Era, in order to rescue Arthur after he had been unceremoniously marooned there. That wasn't something that was easy to forget.

After a few more swipes and taps on the screen, Arthur finally selected "New York City: June 4th, 1983" and stepped back.

"The first thing we'll do when we get to the city is locate the subway. New York City is a large and chaotic place to navigate, so the subway is the fastest way to get around."

Cole watched as the air in front of them abruptly slit down the middle and folded open, revealing a swirling portal on the other side. Father and son glanced at each other, nodded, and then ran and flung themselves through the rippling opening.

Pastel shades of pink, green, and blue flashed quickly past Cole's eyes as he and Arthur sank deeply through the folds of time. Warm air whipped by Cole, tousling his hair, and he laughed loudly, enjoying this unconventional way of traveling. Time travel used to leave him feeling disoriented and nauseous, but once he was able to adjust himself to the process, it quickly became an exhilarating experience.

A bright white light suddenly bloomed beneath them and swallowed them whole. They were spit out through a portal and appeared inside a cramped bathroom stall. Arthur landed gracefully on his feet, but Cole wasn't so lucky -- his right boot sank deep inside a toilet bowl. "*Ugh*! You couldn't have programmed the entrance to be inside a warm café or something?" he groaned, pulling out his soggy shoe and shaking it dry.

"Sorry, Cole. *The Astrolabe's* tracking system randomly assigns the entrance locations. I think it makes things more exciting!"

He suddenly held up a finger to his lips and they fell silent, listening intently. Someone had just entered the bathroom.

"Where are we?" Cole whispered as soon as the stranger left.

"I think we're in Grand Central Station. It's a railroad terminal," Arthur whispered back.

As soon as they were sure that the bathroom was empty, they opened the stall door and quickly exited the room. A short staircase packed with people led upwards to the main concourse. Cole looked up in awe as he and Arthur ascended the stairs; his mouth fell open in wonder. The main concourse in Grand Central Station was a vast, echoing, palatial chamber. Thousands of people passed through the immense terminal and the roar of their mingled conversations hung in the air like a heavy fog. The shiny floors were carved out of a glossy, tan-colored marble and the matching stone walls rose one hundred and twenty-five feet into the air to meet at the ceiling. Cole's eyes fell on a row of three large windows near the rear of the concourse; images of magnificent cathedrals filled his mind. The domed, emerald green roof that hung over the crowd was covered in drawings of shining constellations. Bright stars danced across its surface.

Circular lamps above them bathed the expansive room in a warm yellow light. On a stretch of wall to Cole's left he saw train information being presented on a black Solari board, a row of displays that were covered with flapping panels. The noise from the panels reminded him of a flock of birds taking flight.

A warm rush of adrenaline began to pump through his veins as he looked this way and that, trying desperately to take in all the various sights and sounds. A large smile stretched across his face. Much like *The Astrolabe,* the spirit of possibility itself seemed to be embedded in Grand Central Station's walls.

Cole hurried to keep up with his father as they pushed their way through the heaving crowds. They passed by a round, 18-sided information booth that had been constructed out of the same tan marble as the floors and walls. It was surrounded by a swarm of people all wearing similar confused expressions on their faces. Cole and Arthur turned and followed the crowd down a wide hallway with a low ceiling.

"Where is this clue supposed to be located?" Cole asked as they arrived in a dark and foul-smelling subway tunnel.

"Well, son, our final destination is a nightclub called Studio 54. Very popular place in its day. Your grandparents are seeing a concert."

"A *nightclub*? But Grandma and Grandpa aren't cool enough to get into nightclubs!"

Arthur laughed loudly. "I know! They certainly never did anything like that when I was growing up. But it's true! And I have reason to believe that that's where the clue is. I'm still not exactly sure what we're looking for, but I'll know it when I see it."

Cole nodded but remained unconvinced.

"Here comes the train. This should be fun!"

As the subway approached, Cole felt like the word "fun" was a bit of an overstatement. The gray, snakelike S subway train screeched to a gloomy halt in front of them and they slowly piled inside with the rest of the commuters. He was immediately struck by the stark nature of their train car. The flickering overhead lights were a murky yellow color, and swirling black graffiti covered almost every surface; the walls, the windows, and the seats were all coated with it. Most of the words were unintelligible except for one that stood out to Cole like a flashing light: "RAGE."

His fellow commuters were either standing or sitting, and their faces seemed to droop and sag, mouths tight from the stress of the city. A young woman with teased, bleached-blonde hair and tiny nylon shorts clutched her purse close to her chest, a look of deep suspicion in her eyes. Cole kept his eyes on the trash-ridden floor and avoided anyone's gaze until he could exit the dispiriting train.

Thirty minutes later, after getting off the S train and switching to the N train, Arthur and Cole finally arrived at the poorly lit 57th Street Station. Cole was pleasantly shocked when he walked by and recognized one of Keith Haring's chalk drawings scribbled onto a stretch of black wall.

Moving out of the station, they stepped out onto a wide street surrounded by towering office buildings that soared into the night sky. The summer air was cool and mild and the sidewalks heaved with passersby. Acrid car fumes and the thick stench of trash hung in the air like a putrid perfume. Overflowing dumpsters sat on every street corner.

"Follow me!" Arthur said, and they turned left and made their way down the crowded sidewalk. Cole was used to maneuvering through heavy crowds, having been born and raised in the bustling metropolis of Mechanica City, but he still struggled to catch his breath as hundreds and hundreds of people wearing acid washed jeans, tight Hawaiian shirts, neon leotards with matching leg warmers and various other pieces of loud clothing passed by him. It took everything in his power to keep his eyes fixed on his father so that he didn't get lost in the crowd – there was so much life to observe.

They eventually paused at a four-way stop and then took a left past a basketball court that was enclosed by brick walls and a chain-link fence. Through the fence, Cole could see dozens of black and brown boys surrounding a large, checkered dance floor that someone had dragged over to the court. Most of the boys were wearing brightly colored parachute pants and Kangol hats. A gray boombox sat next to the checkered dance floor and it was blasting the song "The Message" by Grandmaster Flash and The Furious Five.

Cole paused at the fence to watch them. "Hold on a second, Dad!" he said, waving Arthur over. He was mesmerized by the dancer's fluid movements, the way that they spun and flipped across the makeshift dance floor. He wasn't the only one: four teen girls with matching perms also stood by the fence and watched. One of them shrieked and giggled when a break dancer looked over and winked.

"Wow, these kids are aweso—HEY!"
Before Arthur could finish his sentence, he whirled
around and glared at a haggard mechanical man
standing behind him that was draped in a trench
coat. He held up his dirty hands in defeat: a pocket
watch was dangling from his fingers.
"I-I was just lookin' at it," he muttered.
"Get out of here!" Arthur barked, snatching
the watch out of his hand. The mechanical man in
the trench coat glared and scurried away.
"I should probably wear this around my
neck for the time being. Just to be safe," Arthur
said. His pocket watch was the size of a grown
man's hand and its silver casing sparkled under the
streetlights. This intricate piece of machinery was
the only way to access the entrance to *The
Astrolabe*. Arthur took it with him wherever he
went.
"Hmm...you know, if I just built
another one we'd always have a backup for
emergencies..."
"Dad!" Cole scolded. "You know we can't
do that. You got rid of all of your spare pocket
watches years ago. If you make another one, then
what's to say that you won't just make another one?
And another one? What if they fell into the wrong
hands?"
"OK OK! You're right," Arthur conceded,
holding his hands up in surrender with a wry smile
on his face. They continued making their way down
the sidewalk.
After walking several long blocks, they
passed by a group of prostitutes wearing white
pumps and fur coats and finally came upon the
infamous nightclub. Studio 54 was a flat and
unobtrusive building placed in between a line of

other nondescript office buildings and a seedy parking garage. However, the main entrance was easily identifiable due to the glossy black awning that hung directly above the doors. STUDIO 54 was written in white block letters that glowed and stood out in sharp relief against the characterless surroundings.

A large crowd of people stood in front of the entrance: sweaty, shirtless men in tight jeans leaned on identical sweaty, shirtless men in tight jeans; young women with crunchy and gelled hair, bold makeup, and bright, sparkling dresses spoke animatedly with their girlfriends; suburbanites and college kids and middle-aged Wall Street businessmen mixed and mingled in a frenzied mob. Loud music was pumping through the walls.

"So...what do we do now?" Cole asked.

Arthur looked down at his wristwatch and nodded his head. "Perfect timing! Any minute now your grandparents will walk out of those front doors and wait by the curb."

"And the clue to the password will just...pop out at you?"

"That's the idea, yes!" Arthur replied, as if this was a perfectly reasonable answer. He moved to stand next to a graffitied newspaper vending machine and Cole followed him. A tall street lamp beamed a sickly yellow light down upon them.

Five minutes crawled by. Arthur bounced on his heels, practically buzzing with anticipation. Cole observed the partygoers standing in front of the club and marveled at their effervescent energy as well as their outrageous clothes. The smells of cannabis and stale beer floated heavily in the air. One woman screamed in shock as her boyfriend pulled down her shirt and exposed her breasts to everyone standing nearby. There was raucous laughter and scattered applause.

"There they are!" Arthur gasped. He pointed at a young couple that had just paused by the curb in front of the nightclub. Cole's grandfather, Marshall, was wearing a denim jacket, a plain t-shirt that had been tucked into his pants, and his hair was coiffed and combed to the back of his head. His grandmother, Susan, had on high-waisted Jordache jeans, a large, white button-down shirt with rolled-up sleeves, and a grey knit vest. A small purse hung from her shoulder.

"They...They look so *young*. Your grandparents were a handsome pair, weren't they?" Arthur asked cheerfully. But Cole couldn't speak. He was reeling with shock from this moment. Here were his *actual* grandparents -- in the flesh! It no longer mattered that they had passed away years ago. They were standing right there in front of him, and, right now, they were happy and full of life.

Time travel is amazing!

Marshall lit a cigarette and put his arm around Susan, his face inches from hers. They laughed and whispered in each other's ears. It was obvious that these two were very much in love -- they couldn't keep their hands off each other.

"I wish I had known them when they were this age," Cole said, sighing deeply.

They continued silently observing them for several more minutes, waiting for a clue to materialize and jog Arthur's memory. Suddenly, the large crowd in front of the Studio 54 entrance started shouting excitedly. When the crowd finally parted, Cole noticed that everyone was staring at a young woman and her male companion. Her blonde hair was slicked back, and she was wearing a denim vest and skirt, a studded belt with the words BOY TOY written on it, heavy bangles and bracelets around her wrists, and several crosses around her neck. Her companion was tall and wore a plain white t-shirt rolled up at the sleeves and heavy eye makeup. His curly blonde hair and soft features gave him a boyish look.

"Um...Dad? What concert did your parents meet at?" Cole asked. His mind was beginning to buzz. *Is that...?*

"I think they met at an early Madonna concert or something."

"DAD!" Cole yelled in excitement. "WHY DIDN'T YOU SAY ANYTHING EARLIER? WE ARE LOOKING AT AN *ICON OF THE MUSIC INDUSTRY!!!*"

"I'm sorry! I never really listened to her music!" Arthur replied, chuckling.

Self-confidence beamed out of Madonna's eyes like blasts of pure sunlight. Raw sexuality dripped off her like beads of water on a raincoat. Cole recognized the young man that she was with as Martin Burgoyne, her roommate. His heart sank when he remembered that Martin would die from AIDS in just three short years...

Madonna threw her head back and laughed, white teeth shining, drinking deeply of the adulation from the admirers that surrounded her. After mingling for five more minutes, Madonna and Martin waved goodbye and walked down the sidewalk to go visit another nightclub.

As soon as they left, the crowd started to break up. Arthur continued staring anxiously at Marshall and Susan.

"So...anything yet?" Cole asked. He glanced at his wristwatch.

Arthur shook his head from side to side. "Uh. Not yet. But it should be any second now..."

Marshall suddenly leaned in and planted a long, passionate kiss on Susan's lips. They rested against a mailbox and melted into each other for several long seconds, oblivious to anyone around them. Cole cringed with embarrassment and was tempted to look away, yet there was something undeniably sweet about the exchange. When Marshall pulled away, he took a deep breath and joyfully shouted out, "HOLY SMOKES!" while thrusting his fist into the air. Susan blushed and giggled. Then he put his arm around her shoulder and led her gently down the sidewalk.

"That's it!" Arthur exclaimed.

"Wait, really? What happened?" Cole asked, furrowing his brow in confusion.

"The answer is 'holy smokes!' How did I forget that?! Mom and Pop would...would always tell that story, the story of how Pop yelled that after their first kiss." He kept his eyes fixed on the curb that his parents had just vacated, lost in thought. A blank expression fell over his face and he lapsed into a long and heavy silence.

Cole stared at him with concern. He noticed that his father's right hand was shaking again, much as it had done for the past six months. After a beat, he cleared his throat uncomfortably.

"Dad? Is everything okay?"

Arthur said nothing. He continued to stare blankly at the curb across the street.

"Dad? Hello?"

Arthur abruptly shook his head and slowly emerged from his reverie. There were tears in his eyes.

"Sorry! It's stupid. I...I just miss them. That's all. Seeing them like this...it's overwhelming. Growing up, my parents had to work all of the time. We never had any money and so, subsequently, there wasn't much laughter in our house. I like seeing them this way. During less stressful times. I...I hate that I wasn't there when they passed away."

Cole felt his heart sink. He opened his mouth to speak, yet no words would come out. What was there to say? He was able to rescue his father two years ago, but he could never bring back the time that his father had lost. He couldn't fix this for him, and that made him feel helpless. But that didn't mean that he would stop trying.

Unsure of what else to do, Cole placed a comforting hand on his father's shoulder. Arthur hastily wiped a stray tear from his cheek and then father and son turned away from the nightclub and made their way slowly back to Grand Central Station.

CHAPTER TWO

They stepped through a floating white door with stained glass windows at the top and found themselves back inside Arthur's laboratory. Sergeant D'Nozo followed closely behind them into the room. Arthur pointed the pocket watch at the door and it closed with a low thud. This door, the main entrance to *The Astrolabe,* used to be stationed beneath Cole's school, but a year ago Arthur decided to move it to this more central location.

The laboratory was as large as a school gymnasium. The walls were covered with striped, cream wallpaper and long shafts of golden light streaked across the wooden floor from a line of square windows. Many complex and intricately detailed inventions, such as a bulky grey cube draped in glowing tubes, along with a large glass cylinder that smoked and vibrated, cluttered the interior of the room. Wooden tables and cabinets took up the rest of the space.

"Sergeant D'Nozo!" Arthur said. "Thank you again for your discretion." He walked over and shook hands with the bodyguard.

"Of course. As always, if you decide to use *The Astrolabe* again, contact the Head of Presidential Security and they'll send me out." D'Nozo gave a sharp nod and marched out of the room.

As soon as D'Nozo left, Arthur's smile vanished and he breathed a sigh of relief. "Thank God he's gone. I'm sick of him."

"What? Why? D'Nozo seems OK. He never tells anyone what we really use *The Astrolabe* for. You pay him off, remember?" Cole replied.

"It's not even that. Why do I even have to pay him off in the first place? It's ridiculous! I'm a grown man! Why do I need a babysitter in order to use my own invention?"

"Well, Dad, you built something *incredible*. And kind of scary. I mean, I'm certainly still nervous around *The Astrolabe*. *Of course* the government is going to want to monitor it."

Arthur chuckled and shook his head. "Come now, son, there's absolutely no reason to fear *The Astrolabe*."

"Weren't you the one who wanted to shut it down two years ago?" Cole asked pointedly.

"Well...um, well, that was two years ago. I changed my mind," Arthur said sheepishly. He blushed. "Listen -- my train is a wonderful (and safe) tool that could be used to aid in expanding our society's collective knowledge. There are so many possibilities. For God's sake, it's a gift to humanity! There shouldn't be any restrictions on it."

"Well, the knowledge that we've obtained from it hasn't all been good..." Cole mumbled. He shuddered as the memory of a transparent, floating beast with ridges running along its massive back filled the forefront of his mind. "I'm still surprised at how lenient President Carver has been about *The Astrolabe*. She easily could have shut it down and banned you from doing more research, but she trusts you. I guess it doesn't hurt that we *literally* saved Mechanica City, after all. If it remains a secret and we clear all trips beforehand with the Department of Homeland Security, then the government won't interfere."

"Yep. That sounds like oppression to me," Arthur quipped. "By the way, I added some cool new features."

"Dad..."

"Oh, it's fine!"

"What did you add?"

"Just a few minor adjustments. I made some improvements to the shield generators that surround each train car. Repaired the espresso machine in train car seven. Small stuff. Oh, and I'm working on a computer system that will track other train cars that are in use! It's mainly a safety precaution. I want to be able to keep tabs on where my equipment is."

"OK, well, just be careful. Don't add anything crazy."

Arthur walked over to a tall bookcase that held several small spinning metal inventions. He pulled down a square black safe and brought it over to a long examination table. On the front of the safe was a combination keypad. He typed in the words

HOLY SMOKES and stood back. Cole held his breath. A moment later, there was a sharp clicking sound and the door to the safe slowly opened.

"It worked!" they cheered together.

Tucked inside the safe was a tiny airship model. It had been constructed out of balsa wood and strips of pure silver. Thin strings held up a red cylindrical balloon. Arthur gently picked it up and held it reverently up to the morning light. He beamed with pride.

"It's beautiful!" Cole gushed.

"I remember the exact day that my father and I built this model. It was the Sunday afternoon before my first day of high school. I had asked him for this model for months. But we really had *nothing* in those days. So, when Pop brought it home for me, I was ecstatic. He never told me how he came up with the money to buy it. I never thought to ask. Anyway, I think I'll stick this in a glass case and display it on my desk. Thanks for your help today, son!"

"Of course! OK Dad, I've got to get to class now," Cole said. "See you later tonight?"

"Sure! I'll be here."

Cole waved goodbye and walked out of the laboratory. He made his way down a carpeted hallway and hurried up a glossy wooden staircase, passing by several framed family portraits on the walls, and hurried up to the top floor. The three-story manor house that he and Arthur lived in was warm and richly decorated. All the interior foundational elements had been constructed entirely from warm mahogany: the dense columns in the entrance hall, the exposed beams that crisscrossed the ceilings, and the sturdy walls that were draped with colorful tapestries.

On his way up the staircase he passed by a silver metallic cat. It was curled up in a ball, snoozing pleasantly on a step. "Come here, Sprocket," he said, and the cat opened her eyes, yawned, stretched, and then slinked over to him. He gently scratched her behind the ears before continuing his ascent.

When he got to the third floor, he turned a corner and came upon a long hallway with several wooden doors leading off of it. He chose the closest one on his left and it opened onto an empty spare bedroom. The walls were completely bare and the air in the room was stale and cold. Cole didn't seem to notice. He strode quickly across the room to a square window, unlatched the wooden frame, and pushed it up. Sitting on the floor next to the window was a heavy jetpack. He picked it up, slid it over his shoulders, and pressed a small red button on the shoulder strap. Orange flames suddenly burst out of small twin engines and Cole bobbed up and down in the air, levitating easily. Then, he aimed his body towards the window and flew straight through it and out into the open air. The sky was bright blue, and a frigid breeze was blowing; Christmas was only two weeks away.

Floating directly above the angular manor house was a large bronze blimp with small circular windows built into every side. A thick, black cable ensured that the large aircraft remained tethered to the roof. Cole had spent the entire summer designing and building it with his father and his father's coworkers, and it now served as his very own one-bedroom apartment. In his eyes it was one of the most beautiful things that he had ever seen.

Cole flew straight up through the brisk winter air and landed softly on a wooden platform that protruded from the bottom of the blimp's main entrance. The morning sun was blazing high in the sky and its warmth was energizing. He turned off the jetpack's engines, took a key out of his pocket, fit it into the lock, and let himself inside.

The interior of the apartment blimp was open and inviting. Across from the front door was an area that Cole had designated as his bedroom. His bed, along with a bedside table and a dresser, had been squished into a corner next to a window. To the left of his bed sat a large plaid couch that was covered in thick, comfortable cushions. A small table had been plopped in front of it. The space across from the couch had been converted into a small kitchen. Bulky, modern appliances had been brought in to complete the space. Cole had made sure to leave just enough room to host intimate dinner parties.

As he was setting down his jetpack, there was suddenly a sharp tap at one of the windows. He turned to see a black drone hovering just outside of the glass -- the mail had arrived! He moved to the window and opened it, allowing the postal service drone to fly inside. It hovered over the kitchen table like a large beetle, dropped off a handful of letters, and flew out of the window again.

Cole snatched up the stack of mail and began to quickly thumb through the letters, his heart racing. Among the stack of bills, upcoming election announcements, and ads for local food festivals, he finally found what he was looking for: a letter from the auspicious aerospace manufacturer Technicus Incorporated. Technicus In corporated was an aerospace firm that specialized in renewable resources. They were champions of exciting and innovative ideas with a focus on creating aviation designs that were environmentally friendly. The company had only been open for five years, but they had already established a well-respected name for themselves in Mechanica City.

He hurriedly tore the letter open and pulled out the contents:

Dear Mr. Bennett,

Thank you for your interest in Technicus Incorporated! After carefully reviewing your resume and speaking with your father, we are interested in moving forward with a formal interview. We have an opening at 10:00 AM on January 5th, 2030. Please contact our offices if you have any questions or concerns. We look forward to seeing you then.

Warmest regards,

Philomena Fallowback

Director of Aviation and Defense Systems

A warm and sickly feeling of dread filled Cole's stomach. He put the letter on his bedside table and sat down on the edge of his bed, feeling a conflicting mixture of elation and trepidation. He knew he should feel more enthusiastic about this exciting news, since he was a big fan of the company and had followed them for years, yet jagged shards of stress and anxiety held him back. His father's face suddenly swam to the front of his mind and his stomach tightened into knots. A week ago, during dinner, Arthur had excitedly mentioned that a designer position with Technicus Incorporated would become available over the summer and he was pushing for Cole to get the job. At the time, Cole had seemed interested in the offer. He loved his father and was very grateful to have his help with job prospects.

But that night, as he lay in bed staring up at the ceiling, he let go of what he was "supposed" to be feeling and allowed his true feelings to crash over him. Time suddenly felt like it was accelerating, faster and faster, and he was struggling to keep up. Every aspect of his life was finally in perfect balance: his relationship, his friendships, and his family. Why would he want anything to change? He didn't want to think about it. *Plus*, he thought to himself, *how can I survive at such a professional company like Technicus Incorporated when I feel like an inept child half the time?*

After several minutes of tense silence, Cole decided to put the letter in a drawer in his bedside table and try not to think about it. At least until after the holidays had ended. There was no reason to let this impending job interview ruin his Christmas.

After quickly changing into gray slacks, a white button-down shirt, and a newsboy cap, Cole slung his messenger bag over his shoulder and was ready to head to class. Before he left, however, he pulled down a long periscope that hung from the center of the apartment blimp and peered into the viewer. It looked out over the sparkling and multitiered Mechanica City skyline. A warm feeling of joy bubbled up in his chest. Dozens of skyscrapers pierced the azure sky, reflecting brilliant shades of gold and silver that twinkled in the morning sunlight. If he turned to the left to look northward, he could see the statuesque stone building of St. Cajetan's Cathedral, and then further along he spotted the top of the newly re-built Empress Hotel. He took in all the dirigibles and blimps that sailed through the air, delivering passengers to their various destinations.

Today is going to be a good day, he thought happily.

If he looked even farther out into the distance, he could just make out a tiny neighborhood that resided on the outskirts of the city called Figgenbottom. He could see the pointed roof of Belding Manor, a stuffy Victorian boarding house that he used to live in. The landlord was an austere middle-aged woman named Madame Carmichael. She was vindictive, money-hungry, and just so happened to be his aunt. His departure from the boarding house hadn't gone very smoothly and he hadn't spoken to her in two years. He planned on keeping it that way.

He looked down at his wristwatch -- twenty minutes to spare. He hoisted the jetpack over his shoulders again and flew back down to the manor house.

.

CHAPTER THREE

Cole stepped out of the front door of the manor house and made his way down the icy sidewalk. Every few feet he would pass by thick clumps of melting snow, the only remnants left of a snowstorm that had enveloped the city a few days before. He lived with his father in the very center of downtown Mechanica City, in an area called the Buronzo District. The manor house sat on a busy stretch of road named Argenti Avenue.

The city was alert and energized that morning, rushing by him on all sides. The citizens of Mechanica City were bundled up in heavy furs and long coats to block the winter wind that whistled between the skyscrapers. Lucy's Diner, the most popular brunch spot in downtown Mechanica City, had its heated patio thrown wide open for the crowds that had braved the winter cold; a long line wrapped around an entire city block. Cole pulled up the collar of his jacket and continued walking.

He eventually passed by a lively, mid-sized plaza called Leonardo's Square. Fifteen large Christmas trees stood in a long row, each one for sale, and the small stores inside the plaza were draped with festive garland and twinkling lights. A tiny silver dirigible hovered above the plaza and showered fake snow onto the shoppers below.

Cole walked two more blocks before Brume University finally loomed up ahead. It looked the same as it always did: lofty academic buildings in a pentagon shape surrounding two identical brick buildings that stood in the center of an expansive green campus lawn. Winding brick pathways connected each of the academic buildings.

A vibration suddenly buzzed inside his pocket, so he paused at the curb in front of the campus entrance and pulled out his phone. A headline written in bold, swirling script scrolled across the glass face of the phone: "ROGER SIMPSON BECOMES FIRST MECHANICAL MAYOR OF MECHANICA CITY!"

"HELL *YES!*" Cole yelled. He jumped up and down and thrust his fist into the air, his heart soaring at this news. Roger Simpson's historic campaign had been a major story for the past year and Cole, much like everyone else in Mechanica City, had followed every second of it with intense interest. He was handsome, charming, and charismatic, and the media followed his every move. Cole had been more than happy to turn in his vote for Roger during the previous day's election.

As he passed underneath the wrought iron entrance gates to Brume University, a group of students on their way to class walked by and greeted

Cole with a wave. They were bundled up in heavy coats and their warm breath rose in thick plumes in the cold air. He entered the Engineering building and made his way down the crowded hallways. A warm flush of familiarity and excitement coursed through his body as he walked into the AeroTech lecture hall. This was his favorite place on campus, maybe in the entire city, and he was anxious to get to work.

The first person that he spotted was, unfortunately, his nemesis Bianca Cheswick. The two had been enemies ever since their first day at Brume University four years ago. She had bullied him relentlessly, angered by the unfounded belief that Cole had bought his way into the AeroTech program (never mind the fact that her father was an oil tycoon and she was one of the youngest students to ever get accepted into the program.) She was finally forced to stop, however, after Cole caught her stealing exam answers and threatened to expose her to Professor Khan unless she left him and his friend Olivia alone. She had begrudgingly agreed, and they hadn't had any issues since then.

Bianca's lip curled when their eyes met. However, she held her tongue and went back to staring at her phone. Cole ignored her and moved on. His friend Olivia was sitting in the first row of seats and she energetically waved him over.

"Good morning, Cole!" she said. Long box braids fell to her shoulders. On her desk sat a bright red French Press along with a porcelain mug. She pushed down the plunger and poured herself a steaming cup of fresh coffee. Then, with a sigh, she put the mug to her lips and drank deeply.

"Did you see the news about the new mayor?" Cole asked excitedly as he sat down next to her.

"I did!" she responded. "I can't believe how quickly things have changed around here! Did you know that my parents, who usually aren't political at all, actually went out and canvassed for..for..hiscampai-?" She opened her mouth wide and released a large yawn.

"It looks like you really need that coffee this morning," Cole quipped. He noticed heavy, dark circles hanging under her eyes. She sagged sleepily in her seat.

"This month is trying to kill me. Actually, scratch that -- *senior year* is trying to kill me," she said, laughing. "I was so excited when they told us that we would be taking less classes this year. Then our remaining classes just doubled the workload, so..."

The doors to the lecture hall suddenly burst open and their instructor, Professor Khan, strode boldly into the room. The bright, encouraging smile that she wore every day was once again on full display that morning. She was wearing an emerald green hijab, a brown aviator jacket, and leather lace-up boots. Thick goggles rested on her head.

"Good morning, senior pupils!" she said to the class. Pausing to stand in front of her desk, she stood up straight and saluted her students. Everyone jumped to their feet and saluted back to her.

"Now for today's lesson, which I'm *very* excited about. We'll continue our focus on orbital mechanics. Specifically, measuring the impulse per unit that is needed to land on a foreign planet." She waved her hand over the top of her desk and a glass screen unrolled behind her. "Can anyone explain the Hohmann transfer orbit to me?"

As usual, Bianca's hand shot into the air. She answered without being called on. "The Hohmann transfer orbit is used to move a spacecraft between two circular orbits with different radii that are revolving around the same planet."

"Precisely, Bianca! However, there is some controversy surrounding this method. Can anyone tell me why this might be considered an imperfect method of calculating planetary movement?"

"It neglects to include the planet's own gravity and, therefore, gives you very inaccurate readings for burn timings," Bianca answered again. She took a moment to look around at the rest of the class with a smug look on her face.

"Right again! So, what should one do in this situation? Does anyone other than Bianca know?"

The class remained silent.

"Well, this is where the Patched Conic Approximation comes into play. A much more effective option."

For the next hour, Professor Khan continued with her lecture while her students dutifully scribbled down notes with their various note-taking devices. Around the thirty-minute mark, Cole's hand started cramping up painfully. He winced but continued to write.

"And as I always say, your goal should always be to reduce an n-body problem to multiple two-body problems. So! Now that we've had a chance to cover the Patched Conic Approximation, I expect a six-page essay on change-of-plane thrust and its relationship with velocity vectors by Friday," Professor Khan said. The entire class groaned.

"Alright, that's enough," she chided good-naturedly. "Now, if everyone would please stand. The time has come for another trip in The Battle Simulator!" She motioned towards an enigmatic door that was covered by a red velvet curtain. A student with a crooked smile named Carter *oohed* with excitement and the class laughed. Professor Khan smiled patiently.

"Yes, Carter, it *is* very exciting. Now, two months have passed since you last experienced The Battle Simulator. I expect some of you to be a bit rusty. However, I'm confident that my senior students will adapt quickly and pull through. Line up in front of the door, please."

Everyone hurried out of their seats and rushed to stand in front of the doorway. Cole and Olivia stood next to each other and smiled, humming with anticipation. Professor Khan pulled a golden tassel and the thick velvet curtain dropped and fell to the floor. A wooden door with strange and swirling markings on its face revealed itself and then slowly opened on its own.

Dim red light poured down on them like haze as each student passed through the door and stepped into a cramped antechamber. They all picked a glowing white plastic bodysuit from a line of suits that hung from hooks on each side of the antechamber and put them on over their clothes. The plastic material molded itself tightly around their bodies and released any excess air with a slurping sound.

"Now, I feel the need to make this gentle reminder once again," Professor Khan said, looking pointedly at Carter. "Please keep *all* of your limbs inside the simulation pod. At all times. It may feel real, but this is only a simulation."

Cole's thoughts slipped back to the very first time that he had entered The Battle Simulator. It was during his sophomore year and the simulation had been equal parts exhilarating and nerve-wracking. The objective of the simulation was different every time; sometimes you had to connect giant holographic metal pieces together to build an aeroship in under fifteen minutes, while other times the objective was to match the correct propulsion system to a series of specific aircrafts and then observe their flight patterns. The Battle Simulator was an incredible piece of technology and Cole felt deeply proud that he was one of the few that got to experience it.

As soon as everyone was dressed in their bodysuits, they lined up in front of a metal door that had suddenly appeared at the back of the antechamber. It slid open and thick white smoke poured into the room. Cole's classmates passed through the smoke and entered a different room that was full of egg-shaped simulation pods dangling from the ceiling in rows. Everyone chose one at random and climbed inside.

Cole stepped into a simulation pod, laid back on a cushion, and entered his student number into a keypad that had materialized onto the glass case above him. It dissolved and was replaced with a list of simulation levels to choose from. Each of them was grayed out except for one: Space Chase. He slid a pair of goggles down over his eyes, pressed the Space Chase icon, and experienced the now familiar sensation of his body being pulled and stretched in every direction. His vision faded to black. A few seconds later, his surroundings crackled and flickered back into view: he was now inside the cramped cockpit of a small spacecraft. His legs were bent uncomfortably at the knees. A small earpiece was tucked inside his ear.

Cole's eyes bulged in shock as he looked around and assessed his new surroundings. Outside of the window in front of him was nothing but dense black space, a thick, silent blanket of darkness that was dotted with stars. It stretched out endlessly in every direction. Off in the distance, roughly two hundred yards away, was a large red planet whose surface churned with turbulent, swirling storm clouds. A bright holographic starting line bobbed up and down in the air.

On either side of him were long lines of floating spaceships that were the same model as the one that he was sitting in, the tips of their long aluminum wings nearly touching each other. Each ship held one of Cole's classmates. He could see that they were all wearing similar expressions of nervous excitement.

"Attention! Welcome to Space Chase. You will have exactly thirty minutes to complete this simulation," came Professor Khan's voice from inside Cole's earpiece. "When the starting line disappears, race your aircrafts towards Genesis 6, the red planet that you see in front of you, and land it safely on the planet's surface. A simple objective, right? Wrong. Enemy aircraft surrounding the planet will do everything in their power to attack you and bar your way. Utilize all your training to make it safely to the planet's surface. Understood? Good luck!"

Cole took a deep breath and gripped the steering wheel with sweaty palms. Anticipation burned sharply in his chest. He quickly ran through the pages and pages of notes that he had taken on flight dynamics but, strangely, he came up empty.

All the information seemed to have poured out of his mind like a malfunctioning faucet.

The starting line suddenly flashed three times and faded away. Cole pressed the throttle button on the dashboard and he was thrown backwards as his spaceship jolted forward; the speed on the spaceship was unbelievable! The angular, silver spaceships floating next to him followed suit, blasting swiftly through the black sky, their twin engines generating bright plumes of fire.

Everyone steered their ships with wild abandon, twirling and flipping through the air, pushing the throttles almost to their breaking point. A sandy haired boy named Harrison, one of the more skilled pilots in the class, rammed the bow of his ship roughly into any spacecraft that was in his way until he pushed to the front of the class. Cole swerved his ship to the right and swiftly dodged the chunks of smashed aluminum that now littered the air, the remnants of the spaceships that had been damaged in Harrison's wake.

But Harrison didn't stay in first place for long -- things ended just as quickly as they had begun. Olivia, like a stealthy jaguar stalking its prey, dipped underneath him and then abruptly changed direction, steering her spaceship up and ramming its nose into the underside of Harrison's ship. There was a loud crunching noise and his ship went spinning wildly off course, thick plumes of smoke pouring out of the engines. Cole cheered with exhilaration at Olivia's ingenious maneuver and continued to steer his ship straight ahead.

He streaked past four silver spaceships and sped onwards, the swirling red storm clouds rushing up to meet him as the planet loomed larger and larger. The blood was pounding in his ears and he vibrated with excitement. This was easy! He swerved sharply to the left, sharply to the right, and then barrel rolled over two spacecrafts that had gotten their wings stuck together.

A large shadow suddenly passed in front of the surface of Genesis 6. Cole's stomach dropped: a long line of ominous black spaceships suddenly materialized in front of the red planet. Each spacecraft was nearly seventy feet wide and, in Cole's mind, resembled an immense shard of jagged, obsidian coral. Gun barrels were cocked and pointed straight at the students.

Cole only had a second to flip the switch to his spaceship's shield before neon green blasts of scorching hot energy burst forth from the front of the enemy line and slammed into his classmates. Chaos erupted in the air. One of the blasts smashed into a small cluster of spaceships flying to the right of Cole and they all exploded at once, creating a massive fire ball of liquified metal that sank down to the infinite black expanse below.

He darted through the air, dodging green energy blast after green energy blast, flipping upside down to avoid the onslaught of explosions. Wreckage from dozens of destroyed spaceships littered the sky and pelted the sides of Cole's spacecraft. His hands white knuckled the steering wheel. Panic flowed through his body as he darted in and out of enemy fire, trying everything he could to keep his spaceship stable and make it past the battalion.

Keep going. Keep going! You're almost there!

After several tumultuous minutes, he finally broke through the line of enemy spacecraft and sailed through the planet's atmosphere. Adrenaline pumped painfully through his veins and he suddenly couldn't seem to catch his breath. With shaking hands, he turned off the shield and tried to take several deep, steadying breaths. Bursts of white-hot anxiety rolled through him like a massive wave striking a beach over and over again. Dark spots began to dapple his vision. *What is happening to me?* Slapping his cheeks or shaking his head did nothing to help him regain focus.

Cole's ship continued descending through the dense atmosphere. Thick clumps of red clouds and fog whipped by and obscured his vision. He flicked on the headlights at the front of the ship, but they barely pierced through the cloudy atmosphere. The surface of the planet had to be close. He wiped away the sweat that was pouring down his face and struggled to get his breathing under control. *Just keep breathing.*

A sound like nails striking glass suddenly filled the ship and roared in Cole's ears. *What now?* he thought miserably. He looked out of the window and could see sharp objects pelting the roof as well as the sides of the spaceship. With shaking hands, he turned on the wing cameras and what he saw sent a fresh wave of panic rolling over him; heavy showers of silica were pouring out of the clouds and raining down on top of him. The razor-sharp shards of glass ripped through the exposed metal on the ship, puncturing deep holes and slicing wires all over its body. Cole cursed loudly and frantically pushed the shield button. It was too late - - the shield had been damaged and could only feebly flicker on and off.

The spaceship shook roughly from side to side and began to emit a high-pitched whine. Cole screamed; with a loud shriek, the left wing tore clean off the side of the spaceship. Thick black smoke and bright orange flames poured out of the jagged hole where the left wing used to be. He was going down.

Other spaceships loomed out of the fog and appeared on either side of him, racing him to the craggy red surface of the planet. It was rushing up quickly to meet them. If Cole didn't do something soon, he would smash right into the ground. He had no other choice: he pushed the escape button positioned above him and held his breath. Instead of being ejected out of the roof of the spaceship and into the open air, however, he remained rooted to his seat. It wasn't working.

"Oh, shi-" Cole said, and, with one final low whine, his spaceship slammed into the planet's surface. A fiery explosion erupted over the crash site.

Everything around him abruptly slowed down and he was engulfed in darkness. Like a broken TV screen, distorted black and white static filled Cole's goggles and he felt his body being pulled and stretched like malleable dough. When his vision finally cleared, he found himself back inside the simulation pod. He slowly sat up, hot shame burning in his chest. There was no question – he had failed.

As soon as the class returned to the lecture hall, Professor Khan uploaded the final scores onto the glass display board and stepped out of the room. Cole's stomach sank as he looked at his score: tenth place.

"Rough day?" Olivia asked.

"You could say that," Cole replied. "I...I don't know what happened in there. I made stupid mistakes."

"Hey, don't be so hard on yourself," Olivia chided. "You can't be perfect at every simulation. This one was really, really difficult."

"Thanks," Cole answered morosely. His nerves were still frayed. "I'm glad at least one of us made the top three." He stared at her second place score enviously.

They stepped out of the lecture hall together and then parted ways. Cole walked slowly down the hallway, brooding about his score. Why did he have a panic attack? The Battle Simulator could be a stressful experience, but he had never been debilitated by fear before. He hadn't felt like this in years. Was it going to happen again?

Suddenly, his phone vibrated in his pocket and he pulled it out. It was a text message from his best friend Brody:

Drinks at Jules tonight? Bring Gabe!

Getting drunk with Brody at their favorite local gay bar sounded like the *perfect* antidote to this disappointing day. Feeling a bit lighter, Cole made his way to his next class.

CHAPTER FOUR

That night, Cole made his way down to
Tesla Boulevard, the long, tree-lined street that
served as the center of LGBT nightlife
in Mechanica City. The stress of the day was slowly
starting to leave him as he happily strolled down the
street. He eventually turned a corner and came upon
a long line of boisterous gay bars that were squished
next to each other. Glowing neon signs lit up the
long row of bars, with names like Hammerhead,
Tulip, and Exotica. Each building was outfitted with
a bright rainbow flag that flapped in the cold
breeze.

Cole ran across the wide, hectic street and
slipped into a squat brick building. He took off his
coat and looked around. Like most of the gay bars
in the city, Jules was loud, mostly clean, and on the
smaller side. Despite this, it was still Cole's favorite
bar. Stenciled designs of large, black gears covered
the brick walls and a circular bar stood in the middle

of the room. Soft purple track lighting, as well as exposed copper pipes, ran along the ceiling above this centralized bar. Rows and rows of glass liquor bottles with colorful labels sat on a glass shelf. All of these were nice, but the thing that Jules was most known for, its most famous feature, was a large, round analog clock that was fixed to the ceiling. Whimsical illustrations of stars and planets bordered the clock, and it ticked softly above the bar patrons.

He surveyed the crowd for a moment, drinking in the boisterous bar patrons, before finally spotting Brody and Brody's boyfriend, Safi, standing at the bar. They waved him over.

"Hey guys, how are you?" Cole asked. Brody and Safi already had their drinks.

"We're good!" Brody said, raising his voice above the din of the music. "I didn't think it would be so crowded on a Wednesday night!" He smiled pleasantly and took a sip of his drink. Safi, however, waved halfheartedly and stared at the floor. He was tall with dark brown skin, black hair, hairy and muscular arms, and a round stomach.

"Well, let me order a drink and we can catch up. Grab a table and I'll meet you there," Cole said, and Safi and Brody disappeared through the crowd and headed towards the back of the bar.

Cole bought a rum and Coke from a shirtless bartender wearing suspenders and chuckled when he received the glass; thick, white smoke bubbled up out of the top and covered his face. All the drinks at Jules were absurd. But after the frustrations of today, he needed something to cheer him up. He waved away the thick smoke and then headed in the direction that Brody and Safi had gone down.

He found them sitting at a high-top bar table that was next to a stone pillar. The pillar had been wrapped in festive green garland that was dotted with twinkling red and white lights. A small wooden stage with a curtain was positioned at the back of the room. A drag queen named Phyllis Navidad, wearing a hefty blonde wig and a red latex Mrs. Claus dress, was walking through the audience and cracking jokes.

"It feels like I haven't seen either of you in forever," Cole said. "How have you been, Safi?"

"Oh, just fine! Yep. Things are *perfect* now," Safi answered bitingly. He looked away and took a long swig of his drink.

There was a tense pause. Brody flashed his eyes angrily at Safi, but he ignored it. Brody chuckled uncomfortably and plowed ahead with the conversation.

"Y-Yeah, things are great! We've both been pretty busy. It feels *so* good to finally have a night off from homework and rehearsals."

There was another tense pause. The physical space between Safi and Brody was noticeably colder.

"Wait a minute, I just realized -- no boyfriend? Where's Gabe?"

"He couldn't come tonight because he had to work," Cole responded.

"Gross. Well, I'll make sure to drink twice as much tonight to make up for his absence. By the way, we had auditions for the spring musical today and I'm happy to report that I was cast!"

"I never expected anything less. What show are you doing this year?"

"It's called *Of Might and Mettle*. I'm playing a character named Rufus," Brody replied proudly.

"It's a really good part," Safi said. "It *is* the secondary lead role, not the *lead* lead role, but he's perfect for it so it doesn't matter. He'll turn it out!"

"Well, I'm happy for you, Brody. At least one of us is succeeding academically today," Cole said. He grimaced and took a large gulp of his drink.

"What do you mean?"

"I had an exam today in The Battle Simulator. It...did not go well," Cole answered. He recounted the story of the spaceship race simulation, his sudden panic attack, and how defeated he had felt after slamming his ship into the ground.

"I've never been superstitious or anything, but do you think this could be an omen of some kind? What if this is the start of a bad pattern, you know? I mean, the next exam could be even worse! I can't start messing with my GPA now!"

"*Relax*, Cole! You're going to give yourself an ulcer!"

"I know, I know..."

"Are you still seeing that therapist?" Brody asked. Two years before, the summer after his sophomore year, Cole had gone to see a clinical psychologist named Dr. Krumpleton. Between the stress of helping his father adjust back to modern life as well as the many traumatic encounters with Malick, he had some intense emotions that he needed to process. Dr. Krumpleton was very small, very old, and wore round glasses with Coke-bottle lenses. Cole couldn't tell him the specifics of everything that had happened to him that year, but his therapist was a highly intelligent and empathetic man who still dispensed sound advice.

"No, I stopped seeing him six months ago."

"Well, maybe you should go back and see him. It could help! And listen, you've done really well on, like, ninety-five percent of the other simulations that you've completed, right?"

"I mean, I guess. Yeah."

"So, it's only logical to assume that you'll ace the next one," Brody assured him.

"Well...you make it sound so simple. But maybe you're right."

"No, Cole. I *am* right. I'm *always* right."

The curtains in front of the small stage suddenly flung open and Phyllis Navidad stepped out. The song "Dear Santa (Bring Me a Man This Christmas)" by The Weather Girls started blaring from the speakers and Phyllis's glittery red lips lip-synced along to the track. Bursting with charisma, she kicked and twirled around the stage and the boisterous audience ate it up. After gliding around the room to collect her cash tips, she kicked out her right leg and slammed her body to the ground in a death drop. The audience cheered and tossed fistfuls of red and green napkins into the air.

"By the way, is The Straw Hat Society still trying to recruit you?" Cole asked.

Brody scoffed and rolled his eyes. "Yes. Sophia, the current head, still asks me about once a week to be co-head with her but I'm just not feeling it." The Straw Hat Society was an exclusive group of the most talented students in the Drama Department at Brume University. Cole had met some of their members in the past and they were about as elitist and obnoxious as he expected them to be.

"I don't understand why he won't give them the time of day. It's an honor to be a part of it," Safi said.

Brody laughed. "An honor? They never wanted me to join to begin with! Besides, I've clearly proven that I don't need their professional connections in order to be successful."

"Yes, Brody!" Cole laughed. Brody wasn't exaggerating. At the end of his sophomore year, he wrote and starred in *The Astrolabe*, an autobiographical play that retold his part in the circumstances surrounding what was now known in Mechanica City as The Malick Scandal. The show was extremely successful, and ever since then his shows had grown a bit of a cult following on campus. Every time he performed a new one it sold out immediately.

Safi slammed his drink down roughly on the table. "Enough! Brody, can we please stop avoiding the *major event* that will be happening this summer?!"

Cole froze. Brody's face paled and he deflated into his seat. There was a long, strained silence while Safi threw his head back and gulped down the rest of his drink.

"What's going on?" Cole asked.

"Well...I was planning on telling you when I had some more information..." Brody said sheepishly. "I found out some potential good news about this summer."

"Oh?" Cole said. "Like, after graduation?"

"Yeah. My friend Jessica – you remember Jessica Chen, right? -- lives in New York City. She called me a few days ago and, apparently, she's going to need a roommate at the end of July. I...well...I might agree to live with her! She also said that she'd be able to get me a day job so that I can start auditioning for shows right away."

"New York City?" Cole said in surprise. "That's crazy, I was actually just there!"

"You were?" Brody asked suspiciously.

Cole grimaced and kicked himself for this slip of the tongue – his buzz was setting in. He flashed his eyes at Brody with a look that pointedly said, "We'll talk about it later."

"Anyway, I thought that you have an internship lined up with Mechanica Repertory Theater this summer?" Cole asked. "Won't they be angry when you tell them that you're moving?"

"No, that ends on the first of July. After that I would be free to move!"

Cole struggled to find something to say in response. *Brody is...leaving?* He sipped his drink in silence. Safi leaned back in his chair angrily and crossed his large arms across his chest.

"Guys, this is good news. You should be excited!" Brody pleaded. He stared at them with beseeching eyes, practically begging them to give him their blessing.

"I *am* excited, I-I'm just a little surprised," Cole finally managed to choke out. "I didn't know that you wanted to leave the city." His stomach suddenly felt like he had swallowed fistfuls of sand, but he forced an encouraging smile onto his face.

"It's not that I necessarily *want* to leave, but this potential opportunity has started to make me rethink things. I mean, I've lived in Mechanica City for my entire life! I've never been on my own or away from my parents before. Maybe it's time to at least be open to new possibilities, you know?"

"New possibilities are great, Brody, but what about our plans? I thought that you wanted to start your own theater company here! Like, am I crazy?

Cole, back me up here," Safi griped. He looked like he was on the verge of tears.

Cole remained silent and stared awkwardly at the floor. He wasn't exactly eager to step into the middle of this lover's quarrel. Brody moved closer to Safi and placed a comforting hand on his cheek.

"Listen, babe, I haven't made a decision yet. Who knows what will happen? We're only halfway through the school year. There's no reason to worry about this, OK?" he said, making a valiant attempt at remaining positive. Cole could sense that it was an effort, though.

There was another silence. Safi and Brody stared at each other intensely, as if they were communicating telepathically. Cole finally couldn't take it anymore -- it was time to change the subject. "New conversation topic, okay? It's been a stressful day. For all of us, apparently. Can't we just drink and dance and think about happier things?"

"Sorry! You're right, you're right," Brody agreed. "This is boring. The ice in my drink has already melted and I haven't even danced with Phyllis Navidad yet!"

A thumping electronic beat suddenly started playing through the speakers. Brody's eyes lit up with excitement.

"That's the new The Great Roderigo song! Come on!" He jumped out of his chair, grabbed Safi's hand, and dragged him onto the dance floor. Cole gulped down the rest of his drink and ran after them.

Groups of men and women on the dance floor twisted and moved their bodies together to the thumping beat. Cole, Brody, and Safi laughed loudly and danced around each other, feeling tipsy and buoyant, narrowly avoiding a collision with the rest of the sweaty people dancing next to them. For the rest of the night, Cole smiled and floated along with the pounding music and the twinkling lights.

Later that night, as they stood outside of the bar, Cole hugged Brody and Safi and then headed back to his house. Slightly stumbling down the dark and silent cobblestone streets, the buoyant mood that he had cultivated in the club gradually plummeted. Now that he was away from the lights and noise of Jules, the impact of his earlier conversation with Brody began to course through him. His emotions were scrambled and confusing -- on the one hand, he was elated for Brody. New York City seemed like an incredible opportunity. He didn't know very much about day-to-day life there, other than what he had seen when he visited with his father, but if anyone could live and thrive there it was Brody. Plus, almost all of Brody's former classmates had moved there after graduation.

But on the other hand, Cole was slowly beginning to realize that his college experience was coming to an end. In just a few months, all his friends would graduate and leave Mechanica City behind to start their lives, like tiny seeds tossed in the wind. How many more nights of fun would he have with Brody? There never seemed to be enough time anymore.

CHAPTER FIVE

A week later, Cole woke up to tall clumps of bright white snow piled on his windowsill. The temperature had dropped significantly overnight. He shivered, pulling his blanket around him, and moved to close his apartment window.

After a quick shower, he threw the jetpack over his shoulders and stepped outside, breathing in the sharp, cold air. A gust of cold wind blasted against his face, making his eyes water. It cleared his head and helped prepare him for the day.

Just as he was about to launch himself off the landing platform, something strange caught his attention. Something intrusive and out of place. His eyes had fallen onto the front door of the manor house far below and there was his father, standing in the doorway. But that wasn't the strange part. The strange part was that he wasn't alone. Standing next to him was a woman with long, dark hair that Cole had never seen before. And they were kissing.

He leaned over to get a closer look at this new development, his mouth hanging open in disbelief, but he miscalculated his footing, and, with a shriek, lurched forward and tumbled off the landing platform. He fell through the air like a heavy stone sinking in a lake.

Arthur and the mysterious woman broke apart and looked up in alarm as Cole fell. He somersaulted, his vision spinning and blurring, grasping desperately for the ignition button on his jetpack. Seconds before he slammed into the ground, his fingers finally wrapped around the button and he pushed it. With a loud roar, bright orange flames blasted out of the twin jetpack engines and he was finally able to right himself. He lowered himself slowly to the ground, landing right in front of his astonished father.

"Um. H-Hello, Dad!" he said, raising his hand to greet them. "How are you this morning? Good? Great! That's great. I'm also doing, um, great. As well."

Arthur and his female companion glanced at each other and chuckled uncomfortably, visibly struggling to think of something to say. Cole waited for their response.

"B-Be careful, son!" Arthur eventually choked out. His cheeks burned bright red and he couldn't look Cole in the eyes.

"Well...alright. I guess I'll just see you later then." He turned and walked through the front gate that surrounded the manor house.

Cole's mind spun with anxious fervor. *Who the hell is that woman? And what was he doing kissing her?!* He walked slowly down the sidewalk as if he was in a daze, not seeing where he was going. After crossing 14th Street, he turned a corner and nearly ran head-first into a long line of customers that were standing in front of a food truck. He gave his head a shake and kept going.

His mother had been gone for many years, but somehow Cole had never considered the idea that his father might want to try dating again. He didn't want his father to be alone forever, but Arthur always seemed too focused on reacclimating back to modern life and his work to even think about dating. He had been through an intense ordeal and his mental state was still fragile.

Why would he hide it from me? We tell each other everything!

For the rest of the day, an onslaught of troublesome and bewildering questions stuck in Cole's mind. Would he really be able to pretend like nothing had happened? The answer was obvious -- no. He needed answers and he needed them soon. It was time to set a trap.

After a long day of back-to-back classes and lectures, Cole left campus just as the sun was setting and stopped at a nearby bodega to pick up a few items for dinner that night. As he walked up and down the crowded food aisles, he sent his father a text message:

Hey Dad, wanna hang out tonight? We can make tacos and watch a movie in the lab!

After getting the OK from Arthur, Cole bought the necessary supplies for taco-making and headed back to the house. When the grandfather clock in the entrance hall struck six o'clock, Arthur finally walked into the house and slowly shut the front door. He held his briefcase limply in his hand and headed straight for the laboratory.

"What a day," he groaned as soon as he walked inside, shoulders sagging with exhaustion, and dropped his briefcase next to a small circular table that was covered in glass beakers. "Three new projects were approved today for my design team. *Three!*"

"That's great, Dad! Just make sure to pace yourself. I don't like mentioning it, but you're not as young as you used to be," Cole said. He was standing in front of a long wooden table that held porcelain plates laden with tortillas, lettuce, cheese, ground beef, and sliced tomatoes.

"So stop mentioning it!" Arthur replied, laughing boisterously. "You'll understand when you start your career. It's not that easy to slow down!"

Cole nodded but didn't say anything. His stomach sank uncomfortably as his mind returned to the letter that was sitting in his bedside table drawer.

"Speaking of your career, any word on the Technicus job?"

"Um, yes, actually," Cole said. "I have an interview after the holidays."

"That's *great!*" Arthur cried. "Fantastic work! It really is an excellent company; I know half the staff! You're going to do great."

"Yeah, thank you for putting in a good word for me," Cole mumbled. He felt very eager to change the subject. "Anyway, what do you think?" He gestured widely at the plates of food.

"Wow, son, this is a great spread. You got everything! And you brought out *The Jolly Mafioso*? That old piece of crap? You've outdone yourself! What's the occasion?" A silver film projector stood in the center of the cluttered laboratory and was playing the first few minutes of the film onto a hanging white sheet.

"Oh, ummm? No reason! Just thought it'd be nice to catch up. We've both been really busy. I have no idea what you've been up to lately." As he handed Arthur his food and started making a plate for himself, the face of the mysterious woman with dark hair bubbled up to the forefront of his mind.

"Up to?" Arthur asked. He sat down on a leather couch that had been moved in front of the white sheet. "There's not much to tell. Swamped with work, like I said. We're working on a few things: constructing a new version of the Edison Blimp that can shrink down to a portable size, a project involving dirigibles that will (hopefully) repair telephone towers, and then we just received a request to design new light-weight jetpack cannisters for the police department. Not sure when I'll sleep in the next six months, but this is important work. By the way, how is school? Is Professor Khan still keeping you busy? I still can't believe that she's your professor. I remember hearing about her when she was first starting out!"

Cole sat down on the couch. "It's the same as it always is. Stressful, but I'm getting through it. Homework. Focusing on passing midterms. What I'm going to wear for the Senior Ball. Then there's graduation and what comes after that. It's a lot."

"Graduation? Cole, that's months away!" Arthur replied, shoving a taco into his mouth. "Besides, all of the 'what comes after' will unfold in the way that it's supposed to. You're a very talented man. You have no reason to worry."

"Yeah, I-I guess. But you really can't help worrying about it, though."

Arthur turned away from the movie and looked at Cole sympathetically. "I know this is a confusing time, and you're right to feel overwhelmed. A lot is going to change after this year. But you just need to remember to take it one day at a time and it will all fall into place. Plus, it should make you feel better that you already have an amazing job opportunity that you're reaching for! You're in a better spot than a lot of your classmates!" He placed a supportive hand on Cole's shoulder and then turned back to the movie.

Cole nodded his head in halfhearted agreement and poked at the food on his plate. His stomach clenched with anxiety and he stayed silent for a few minutes. He appreciated what his father was saying, but he couldn't focus on that topic right now, because, most importantly, he still needed to find the right moment to ask Arthur about that strange woman. It had to happen soon or he would lose his nerve.

"Ooh I love this part!" Arthur said. The black-and-white scene playing on the white sheet involved two men: the protagonist of the movie, a fedora-wearing mafioso with a large stomach, and his brainless and bumbling sidekick. They were standing in front of a wooden jalopy with large sacks of cash in the trunk. The sidekick turned to the mafioso and gleefully asked, "Hey, Boss? Mind if I take a little bit off the top?"

The red-faced mafioso turned, grabbed him by the scruff of the neck, and pulled his fist back, ready to punch.

"You tryna cheat me?!" he bellowed.

"N-No, Boss! Never! I-It was a joke!"

The mafioso abruptly smiled and broke out in raucous laughter. The sidekick nervously choked out, "Ha ha ha. Y-You call the shots, Boss! That's why they call you The Jolly Mafioso!"

Arthur groaned at the wooden dialogue and burst out laughing.

Cole finally couldn't take it anymore. He slowly put down his fork and looked at Arthur. "Dad? Um...so, who was that woman that you were kissing earlier today?"

Arthur coughed heavily, doubling over in his seat. He was unable to speak for several seconds. Cole thumped him on the back three times before he was able to quiet down.

"*K-Kissing*? Me?! Wh-What are you talking about?!"

"I saw you, Dad! I nearly fell on top of her this morning! Who is she?"

Arthur fell silent and stared at the floor. Cole noticed tiny beads of sweat pooling on his forehead.

"Alright. Fine," he finally muttered. He put down his plate of food, paused the movie, and turned to look at Cole. "That was Sabina. She and I are, um, seeing each other."

"She's your girlfriend?" Cole asked brusquely. He felt like his brain was heating up and he struggled to ignore it.

"Well, I didn't necessarily say that --"

"How did you even meet this woman?"

Arthur chuckled nervously. "Sh-She and I met at work a few weeks ago. She was interviewing me for *The Daily Pastiche* and we just, uh, hit it off."

"*A few weeks ago*?! When were you going to tell me about this?" Cole said. His hands were shaking.

"Well, it-it's still a new thing! I didn't want to say anything before I knew if it was serious or not!"

"So is she planning on moving in soon?"

"What? No! Of course not!"

"But we tell each other everything, Dad! Why would you keep this a secret?"

Arthur opened his mouth to speak, closed it, opened it again, and then scowled. "Listen, son. I'm sorry, but this really isn't any of your business. My love life has nothing to do with you. I think I'm entitled to keep some things to myself!"

Without thinking, Cole sprang to his feet and glared at his father, hot anger coursing through his veins.

"Cole, what's wrong? Why are you so angry about this?"

"Because!" he shouted, no longer able to hold back the storm raging in his mind. *"What about Mom?!* She...she didn't die *that* long ago! Doesn't she matter?"

The air seemed to go out of the room. A deeply pained expression rolled across Arthur's ashen face and he let out a long sigh, like he had just been sucker punched in the stomach. He stood up and stared straight at Cole.

"Son...I was trapped in the past for twenty years. *Twenty long years.* I was completely alone. I had no one around me. I had nothing. You have no idea what that's like."

Cole stood there, his chest heaving, waiting to feel a sense of satisfaction at having finally confronted his father. But it never came. At the sight of Arthur's wounded expression, all the anger churning in Cole's stomach disappeared and a heavy stone of shame filled the void.

"Now listen...I love your mother. You know that. I will always love her. For God's sake, I traveled back in time to try and save her! I miss her every day! But that phase of my life is over. It has to be over. I just want to move on and enjoy the time that I have left. Shouldn't I be allowed that?" He groaned and grabbed his hand; it was shaking again.

Cole struggled to think of a response. It was obvious that he had gone too far. His father was right. So, why didn't he feel any better? Why couldn't he completely shake off his anger and resentment?

He sighed and looked at his father. Tears had pooled in Arthur's eyes.

"I...I'm sorry, Dad," he finally muttered. "You're right. You should be able to date whoever you want. That's your business. It was just shocking to see, that's all."

Arthur smiled sadly. "Your mother will always be a part of me. Of us. No one is trying to erase her, okay? You don't have to worry about that." He gave Cole a hug.

"Ok, can we continue watching the movie or did you have any more questions about my love life?"

Cole rolled his eyes and smiled, but the anxious knot in his stomach remained firmly in place.

CHAPTER SIX

Several weeks passed. On a cloudy Friday morning in early January, the sound of an alarm rang out and Cole's eyes flew wide open. Today was the day -- his first major job interview.

Now, Cole was no stranger to job interviews – he had suffered through many in the past. However, none of them came close to feeling as high stakes as this one did. Firstly, this was a full-time, salaried position – very adult. And secondly, Technicus had a formidable reputation. Many of the brightest and most accomplished students from the AeroTech program had graduated and gotten jobs there. They were a modern company, forward-thinking, and had created some of the most maddeningly innovative solar and electric aeroplanes that Mechanica City, as well as the world, had ever seen.

After spending the holidays ruminating about the opportunity, he decided that, whether he felt ready or not, his father had helped get him this interview. He had to at least give this a respectable try.

He opened his closet and looked around, searching for a proper professional outfit. A long line of colorful shirts and pants of all colors greeted him. He had a lot more options to choose from now, ever since his sister Ruby started sending him clothes in the mail that she liked (whether he liked them or not was inconsequential.)

After picking his clothes and hastily taking a shower, he called his friend Karma to get some encouragement and to ease his rising anxiety.

"Cole!" said a pleasant voice. Karma's smiling face suddenly filled his computer screen. She was wearing a tailored white suit and her bright red hair fell to her shoulders. Her blemish-free skin had been constructed out of pale white silicone; the most modern mechanical models were all built this way. Cole had first met Karma several years ago at Belding Manor where she had been employed as the Head Housekeeper.

"How are you doing?"

"I'm doing really well!" she responded. "Swamped with work and martial arts lessons but what else is new? You need to visit me at work! I haven't shown you around the new building yet!" Karma was the founder of the non-profit NAAM, or the National Association for the Advancement of Mechanicals.

"I know, I really need to get over there. School has kept me so busy," Cole said.

"Well, that's to be expected. I can't believe you graduate this year! Where has the time gone?"

"Don't ask me. Time is moving way too fast."

"No! Stop! You're going to make me cry," she cried, chin wobbling. Cole rolled his eyes and laughed.

"OK, topic change, because I simply *must* ask: have you seen your dad's, um, friend lately? What was her name again? Sabina?" Karma asked.

Cole scowled. "No. Dad and I haven't talked about her since we got into that fight. Hopefully I'll never have to see her slobbering all over him again. Ugh."

"Cole, be nice," Karma scolded.

He scowled even more in response.

"Don't give me that look. You need to support your father!"

"*Anyway*, I have my big interview today. Any words of encouragement before I leave?"

"Oh, is that today? Fabulous! Are you nervous?"

"A little, yeah. Actually, a lot. I'm a lot nervous."

"Really? Oh, there's no reason to be nervous. You're perfectly capable of nailing this interview."

"I don't know. Am I really that prepar --?"

"Oh, *stop*. You're going to do great! Try not to think of this as the be-all and end-all of job interviews, though. You'll just stress yourself out. Take a deep breath and let whatever happens, happen. Now, go and kick that interview's butt!"

Cole nodded and a small smile crossed his face. "Thank you for the pep talk, Karma! Have a good day."

Although he now lived downtown, Cole had to utilize the cable car and take it twelve long blocks to the headquarters of Technicus Incorporated. It was crammed with commuters at that time of day, so he was forced to stand in the aisles during the journey.

He was eventually dropped off in front of a towering golden office building that stretched towards the sky, its roof nearly touching the clouds. Even in the faint winter sunlight, the building shone and glittered spectacularly. The word TECHNICUS ran boldly across the front of the structure in large block letters. Cole took a deep breath and walked inside.

The entrance lobby was vast and echoing, with large windows that allowed rays of sunlight to pour inside and bathe everything in a warm light. Crowds of men and women dressed in professional attire moved through the space in dense packs.

Can I really fit in here? Cole wondered.

He checked his watch – ten minutes to spare. He turned and watched an overwhelmed mechanical barista inside a small coffee stand complete drink orders for a long line of customers. Cole briefly had unpleasant flashbacks about working for the coffee shop Crema. He got in line and waited for a drink.

Later, coffee cup in hand, Cole moved to stand in the center of the lobby, taking it all in. He looked straight up: each floor was surrounded by a thick glass barrier. This allowed employees and guests to safely look down onto the bustling lobby below. Each of the ninety-five stories possessed this feature, going all the way up to the dizzying top. Small bronze dirigibles and drones zoomed and whirled in the air just above the busy lobby. One flew right over a woman's head, causing her to jump in surprise.

At the back of the main lobby was a long line of large translucent tubes. People lined up and stepped inside each tube, pressed a gold button, and were sent skyward to their various destinations. Cole, staring open mouthed at these wonders, made his way over to a large marble receptionist desk at the center of the lobby.

"G-Good morning! I, um, have an interview with a Philomena Fallowback." He flashed his biggest smile and tried to ignore his churning stomach.

An older man with thinning hair sitting behind the desk gave him a visitor's badge and called Philomena's assistant to confirm that she was available. After getting the all clear, he pressed a button on his desk and waved Cole toward one of the traveling tubes.

Cole stepped inside a tube and waited nervously. For a moment nothing happened. Suddenly, a large swirling burst of wind filled the clear tube and he was lifted off his feet and into the air. His stomach felt like it had fallen into his knees as he was quickly sucked upwards. He laughed joyfully and watched the main lobby zoom away beneath him.

A few seconds later, Cole was safely delivered to the twentieth floor. He stepped out of the translucent tube and appeared inside a smartly furnished waiting area. One wall was covered in bright flowers and green vines. He walked up to yet another front desk and spoke to a mechanical woman wearing glasses.

"Are you Cole?" she asked. Her silicone face was cold and impassive.

"Yes! Cole Bennett. Excited to be here," he replied.

"Great," the mechanical woman replied, not caring at all. "Please take a seat and Philomena will be with you shortly."

Cole sat down on a cream leather sofa and settled in to wait. He turned his head and noticed a bumblebee pollinating a patch of pink flowers that were growing out of the wall. It felt like a good sign.

Here we go, he thought, nervously drinking his coffee. *Everything is fine. All I have to do is be the best, most perfect version of myself. Easy.*

"We're here to check in for the interview," said a deep voice.

"Dalton and Derek! Nice to see you again. I just love it when former interns decide to remain with the company! You can take a seat," the mechanical receptionist said pleasantly.

Former interns?! Cole whipped his head around and stared at two young men, both of them tall and muscular, with chiseled jawlines and short haircuts, who had just entered the room. They both sat down on a couch across from Cole and stared.

An image of a small child wearing an oversized suit flooded Cole's mind as his heart sank to his knees. *Why do I have to see my competition right before the interview?* He stared at the floor, lost in thought, and wiped sweat from his forehead.

"Mr. Bennett?" came a raspy voice.

Cole was abruptly ripped away from the battle taking place inside his mind. "THAT'S ME!" he shouted, jumping to his feet.

As he stood up, his coffee cup slipped out of his hands and hit the ground, splashing spectacularly across the floorboards as well as his right pant leg. Cole, feeling like he wanted to sink into the floor and disappear, started feverishly wiping off his leg.

"Are you alright?"

A woman radiating haughty glamour stood in a doorway next to the front desk. Cole had never seen a stranger person before. She was tall, with voluminous gray hair piled high on top of her large head. A long duster jacket with puffed sleeves hung off her thin frame, which was made even thinner by a cinched and corseted waist. However, the first thing that Cole noticed was her face. The skin was pulled tight and frozen into place due to what he could only assume was copious amounts of filler and injections. Hard domes of what looked like pale marble, meant to represent human cheeks, protruded from the sides of her face and her lips had been inflated to a comically large size. However, despite it all, she somehow pulled it off.

"I-I'm really sorry about the mess."

"Oh, darling, could you get someone to clean this up?" the woman barked cheerfully at the receptionist. "Now, follow me."

Cole followed the proud woman down a long white hallway, past rows of identical cubicles, and into a large and smartly furnished office. An immense neon blue fish tank, packed with a school of brightly colored mechanized fish, took up much of the left side of the office. It made a soft humming sound.

"Take a seat, sweetie! I'm Philomena Fallowback," the woman said. Her voice was loud and gravelly. Cole shook her hand and sat down in a chair in front of her cluttered desk. She pursed her buxom lips and applied a thick layer of red lipstick before continuing.

"Alright! Well. Let's just get straight to it, shall we? I called you in for an interview today for many reasons, one of which was your impressive resume. Another reason was your father – he had some glowing words about you for my assistant. Cole Bennett, son of the famous inventor Arthur Bennett!"

"Oh, well, I-I don't know about *famous*, but --"

"No no! No need for modesty here! After everything your father has done for Mechanica City? Marvelous, simply marvelous!"

"Well, thank you." His shoulders finally began to unclench. She was a fan of his father! Her enthusiasm greatly eased his anxiety.

"I am curious, though. Why would someone like you want to come and work for Technicus Incorporated? I assumed that you would want to work at Bennett Industries. Quite a shocking development, really."

"Well, I wanted to keep all my options open. And, you know, I applied here because I really believe in this company's mission: sustainable aviation. With the devastating effects of climate change happening every day, this kind of company is needed now more than ever."

"Lovely -- I'm *very* pleased. Very pleased, indeed." She attempted to smile, her stiff cheeks straining from the effort. "However, before we start, may I be honest with you about something a little...*unpleasant*?"

Cole sat up straighter in his seat and bounced his leg nervously. "O-Of course you can."

"Well, I just *hate* to bring up something like this, but I find it *awfully* humorous how the world works sometimes! Did you know that your father fired my uncle from Bennett Industries about ten years ago? Fired him right on the spot." She leaned back in her chair and clasped her painted fingers together.

Cole's smile fell and his stomach sank quickly. During the weeks that he spent on Technicus Incorporated research he had never come across this information. *How did I miss something like that?* he wondered. Would this be held against him? It felt like a cruel joke.

"I-I wasn't aware of that. I'm sure that it was just a simple misund--" he sputtered helplessly.

Philomena stared at him. Then her face stretched into a tight smile and she barked out a raspy laugh. "Ha! I was testing you! I'm sorry, darling, but I couldn't resist. My uncle Gustav is a bumbling fool and an alcoholic. No one in our family was surprised *in the least* when he was fired! It's clear that your father is able to make difficult decisions like any worthy boss. I admire that."

Cole forced out a strained laugh. This was unlike any interview that he had ever been on before. Trying to predict the direction of this conversation was giving him a bad case of whiplash.

"*Well*, that's.... that's really something. What a crazy series of events!" he said.

Philomena nodded slowly, staring into space. She pulled out a golden vape pen from her jacket, took a long drag off it, and then blew out a thick cloud of vapor that smelled like strawberries. Cole waited for her to speak again.

"So! Did you bring copies of your resume?"

"Yes, here they are," Cole answered.

However, in his eagerness to hand the resumes over, he stood up too quickly and his foot got caught on the chair leg. With a loud *thump*, he fell to the floor. The resumes flew out of his hands and went flying into the air, raining down and covering the entire office in sheets of white paper. A few of the pages landed right inside the fish tank.

Flushed with shame and embarrassment, Cole hurriedly collected the papers around the room and handed them to Philomena in a damp and crumpled stack.

"I-I'm *so* sorry..."

"A bit clumsy, aren't we?"

"I promise that I'm not usually like this..."

Philomena reluctantly took the soggy resumes and started looking them over, pursing her plumped lips and taking deep drags off her strawberry-smelling vape. Thick white vapor hovered in the air. Cole started sweating from the effort of trying not to cough.

"Let me quickly go over exactly what it is that we do here at Technicus Incorporated. As you know, we are an engineering firm that specializes in building sustainable and environmentally friendly aircrafts for various markets around the world. There are many different departments here but, if offered a job, you would be working in the Aviation and Defense Systems Department, which I am the head of. I'm looking for a very special and specific candidate who brings something new and exciting to the table. So, what would you say your strengths are? What makes you stand out?"

Cole paused as his spirits sank. He had gone over this exact question several times while preparing for this interview and he had always come up with the perfect response. But something wasn't right today. His mind wouldn't cooperate; he was still trying to recover from his embarrassing fall. *I'm a failure, I'm a failure, I'm a failure.* This interview was quickly going off the proverbial rails.

"Um...um, well....that's a great question," Cole replied, desperately stalling for time. "A very good question, I might add! And, like any good question, it deserves an equally good answer! I...I..."

"Yes?" Philomena pressed. She leaned back in her chair and blew smoke rings into the air.

"I...I feel, um, like I stand out because I work well with people and I...um...am a focused person!" he finally blurted out. His face flushed. *What kind of vague answer was that?!*

"Huh. Interesting," Philomena replied cryptically. "Hmm...well, your grades are excellent. I see here that you've taken some very advanced classes. Ooh, and you completed an internship last year with Bennett Industries. Marvelous! Any volunteer work? Here at Technicus Incorporated, we encourage our employees to be community-oriented and to value service. It's the mark of a quality worker and individual."

Cole gulped. Community service? The AeroTech program had always kept him too busy to do anything like that. His spirits sank even further.

"Um well, no volunteering *per se*. But yes, I-I did complete an internship with Bennett Industries over the summer. You could say that it was relatively service-oriented. I helped the aviation team design an apartment complex dirigible that could be built entirely out of recycled plastic and paper. The idea was to build it in such a way that a person from any socioeconomic level could live in it. We didn't make it to the building phase, but we did create a prototype."

"Well, renewable resources *are* an important part of Technicus Incorporated," Philomena responded.

"I try to stay as green and eco-friendly as I possibly can," Cole said, wringing his hands nervously in his lap. He found Philomena's muted expression indecipherable as she continued to peruse his resume.

"One thing I noticed, darling, is that you never applied to the Mechanica Engineering Department's summer workshop. Tsk tsk tsk! I'm on the board for that event. It's a very popular and competitive program. May I ask why you didn't apply? Or, were you just not accepted?"

A bead of sweat trickled down the back of Cole's neck. He would've loved nothing more than to explain to her that the reason why he never finished his application was because he was too busy traveling through time and saving Mechanica City from total destruction! But, of course, he couldn't say any of that. The secret of *The Astrolabe* could never be revealed.

"Um...well, it's kind of a long story. But yeah, it's because I got sick," he finally said. "*Really* sick. Like, the worst flu that you could imagine. Total bummer. I *definitely* wanted to apply to that internship. And I probably would've gotten in!"

Philomena nodded her head vaguely and continued to smoke her vape pen. She pressed her lips together, like two red rubbery tires, and pulled deeply, lost in thought. Several excruciating minutes of silence passed before she spoke again.

"I see. Well, I think that's it! Thank you so much for coming in. Best of luck."

There was a subtle shift in the room. A concerned expression rolled across Cole's face. "H-Have you made your decision already?"

"We'll contact you," she replied firmly.

"But...But don't you want to hear some of my questions first?"

"Oh, no, I don't think that will be necessary. You can send in the next candidate now." Philomena stood up and smiled her tight and strained smile.

This was supposed to last much longer. That can't be good...

A fluttering sound came from the office window. Cole turned his head and stared at the glass, eyes squinted in confusion.

Nothing was there.

"You can send in the next candidate now," Philomena repeated, motioning her hand towards the door. Cole stood up begrudgingly and there it was again – the fluttering noise! It sounded like a flock of birds was hurriedly taking flight all at once. He turned his head to look again and was surprised to see square sheets of what looked like white paper falling from the sky.

"What is *that*?" Philomena asked in alarm.

A cold shiver of dread slowly crept down Cole's back as he moved towards the window. He felt like he was in a trance -- something wasn't right.

Sheets of paper continued to fall slowly outside, like clumps of ominous-looking snowflakes. With trembling hands, Cole unlatched the window and pushed it up.

A gust of cold wind blew inside and tousled his hair. When he leaned out and craned his neck to the right, he could just make out the underside of a large silver airship that was hovering right above the window. It was circular in shape and had a large fan built into its underbelly. White sheets of paper blasted out of the fan and blew in all directions, raining down on the busy streets below.

Cole picked up one of the sheets of paper from the windowsill and looked at the large black words that were splashed across it:

CITIZENS OF MECHANICA CITY!
Read these words carefully: at this very moment in our city's history, we are dealing with an invasion. At every turn, human beings are being replaced by filthy robots. We have become lazy and foolish, slaves to the will of our weak and ineffective government, by relying on these inhuman creatures for even the simplest of tasks. It's an abomination. Was it the "mechanicals" who created and shaped this world? No. Humans did that.
First, they took the good paying jobs. And now our very own mayor is a robot! What will happen to us when there's nothing left? We need to take back what is ours!
The government may be unwilling to speak the truth, but the enlightened members of Project Hominum are more than willing. Our goal is to reinstate and preserve the rightful superiority of the human race. By any means necessary.
If you want to know more about the truth, visit our website at ProjectHominum.com.
There will be more. You will see us again.

They will not replace us!
#HumansFirst

"Wh-What does it say?!" Philomena asked in alarm.

"I...I'm not sure. But it doesn't seem good," Cole replied quietly. His hands were shaking.

He leaned out of the window again, searching for the silver airship, but it had disappeared. He brought the paper over and handed it to Philomena.

"Oh dear. This is very serious. *Very* serious, indeed. I'm so sorry, Mr. Bennett, but I'm really going to have to ask you to leave my office."

CHAPTER SEVEN

"DISGUSTING! Those letters are absolutely *disgusting*!" Karma cried. Her angry, pale face peered out at Cole from a video chat window on his computer screen.

"What was even worse is that after I left my interview, I saw a few people on the street laugh and then pocket the pieces of paper. I guess to read later? Gross." He shook his head in disbelief.

It was later that day, and Cole was seated inside a cushy booth in a quiet corner of Nautique, a high-end restaurant in downtown Mechanica City that had been built inside an abandoned submarine. He nursed a cup of coffee while completing his homework. The restaurant was brimming with well-dressed and boisterous customers drinking wine and eating their dinner. Waiters in crisp white uniforms hustled to the various tables to take orders.

"And the police still haven't figured out who is running Project Hominum yet. What is taking so long?" He minimized the video chat window and switched over to Project Hominum's website. The home page, while simple, remained effective. It was filled with offensive memes and links to anti-mechanical propaganda.

"Well, the Mechanica City Police Department isn't exactly known for being efficient," Karma replied. "But it's only been a day. Things can change at any moment. Project Hominum...I've never heard of that before."

"Hey babe, did you need more coffee?" came a low voice. A handsome young man with coffee-colored skin, a dark beard, and curly black hair came up behind Cole and placed his hand on his shoulder. A pleasant chill rolled down Cole's spine.

"Thanks, but I probably shouldn't have anymore caffeine," Cole replied, smiling up at his boyfriend Gabe. The newly appointed sous chef at Nautique, Gabe was dressed in his chef's whites, a double-breasted white jacket with matching white pants. Over the past year and a half, he had worked hard to establish himself, working late nights and assisting with creating exciting dishes that kept the Nautique customers coming back for more.

"I just need to cut the new junior chefs and I'll come sit with you. Hey Karma!" Gabe said. He smiled, waved at the laptop screen, and walked back towards the kitchen.

"He is so cute," Karma said, sighing.

"He is, isn't he?" Cole replied, blushing. "Anyway, I had a thought..." He glanced over his shoulder and lowered his voice. "Do you think this could have anything to do with

Malick? Think about it -- he's the only one who would be insane enough to cover the city with bigoted propaganda. Is it possible that he survived?"

Malick, or MAL-1K, was the name of a male mechanical that Cole and his friends had battled and destroyed two years ago. A former disgruntled coworker of Arthur's, Malick had been hired to help him open a wormhole through time. They were eventually successful, but after a floating monster broke through the wormhole and possessed him, Malick became unhinged and set out to raise an army of mechanicals that would rid the world of humanity.

Karma shook her head. "No, it can't be him. He wanted mechanicals to take over, remember? This group hates us. I don't think that this is going to slow down any time soon. Anti-mechanical feelings have been brewing ever since Karma's Act was put into place."

Cole shook his head sadly and sighed. "I don't understand. Why are mechanicals such an issue? They're here, have been here, and they're not going anywhere."

"Well, it's clear that the gala that NAAM is throwing tonight couldn't have come at a better time. We need to be able to further our reach and show every mechanical in this country, and all over the world, that there are people out there who will advocate for them! Karma's Act was a great first step, but it was just that – a first step. There is still a lot of resentment and anger out there. Hate crimes against mechanicals have slowed down but they haven't stopped. Awareness still needs to be made available to the public."

Cole nodded mournfully.

"Well, on that somber note, I have to teach a tai kwon do class, so I should be going. Can we get coffee this week?"

"Absolutely! I'll call you," Cole said. The viewing screen went black as Karma signed off.

A few minutes later, Gabe returned to the table and sat down across from Cole. He looked tired but content. "Finally done! How's the homework coming along?"

"Nearly there. Just a few more pages of this essay to finish." He closed his computer and started putting his things back into his messenger bag.

"Hey, I've been meaning to ask you – how did your interview go?"

Cole groaned and covered his face with his hands. "Let's talk about something else."

"What do you mean? What happened?"

"Well, it was a disaster. Pretty much everything that could go wrong, did go wrong: I spilled my coffee on my pants. I dropped my resumes on the floor. Oh! And then it was interrupted by that airship that was dropping papers everywhere. I was so stressed out that my brain stopped working. I know that I didn't get the job. I sucked." He groaned again and put his head on the table.

"I'm sure you didn't suck! But I will admit...it doesn't sound great. Why were you so stressed out?"

"I don't know! I just felt intimidated. I wanted everything to go perfectly and it just...didn't. I can't do anything right. Honestly, I didn't even want to do the interview in the first place."

"But Cole, that's crazy. You *literally* saved Mechanica City. Why would you feel intimidated by anything?!"

"I don't know what's going on with me. I feel like a mess."

Gabe placed a hand on Cole's hand. "I'm really sorry that you had such a hard time. But maybe you can look at this interview as good practice for the next one! And there *will* be a next one. I mean, there are so many other companies out there that you could *easily* work for. It's like my abuela always says, 'Todos los caminos llevan a Roma.' All roads lead to Rome. You'll still get to where you want to go; it'll just be in a different way. You know what? I have something that will cheer you up."

"What is it?" Cole asked.

Gabe grinned, turned around, and held up his hand. Delbert, the head chef, appeared from around a corner carrying a large dessert on a porcelain plate. Lines of steam rose off a dense slice of chocolate cake that was topped with a generous helping of vanilla whipped cream.

"Is that for us?!" Cole asked excitedly.

Delbert put it on the table, bowed, and walked away.

"It's technically for you, but you know I want a few bites! Dell helped me decorate it. Do you like it?" Gabe handed Cole a fork and he cut a piece of the cake and put it in his mouth. His face lit up.

"I love it! Thank you so much! I really needed this after today." Cole and Gabe smiled at each other and continued devouring the delicious cake.

A few days later, Cole woke up to find a rotten email waiting in his inbox -- a formal rejection from Technicus Incorporated. Philomena Fallowback was gracious and polite and thanked him for his time, but a rejection is still a rejection. Ultimately, his only option was to pick himself up and continue applying. For his next interview, he would have to make sure that he was much calmer.

On a Friday afternoon at the end of January, Cole walked into the manor house and dumped his messenger bag in the entrance hall. It had been a long and arduous day at school; a written exam in his Engineering IV class, a two-hour Chemistry lab, and another trip in the Battle Simulator. His stomach grumbled loudly – he was starving.

Sprocket suddenly sauntered into the room and clanked over to him. She wrapped herself around his ankles and purred softly. He bent down to briefly scratch her behind her metal ears and then made his way towards the kitchen.

As he turned a corner and passed into the kitchen, he suddenly stopped in the doorway, frozen in shock -- Arthur was seated at the dinner table, hands clasped nervously. In front of him was a tall man that Cole had never seen before. And next to this man, sporting a dreamy and unfocused expression on her face, was his older sister Ruby. It took Cole a moment to recover himself.

"Ruby! Wha-What are you doing here?! When did you get back into the city?"

She opened her mouth to reply but the tall stranger talked over her. "We flew into the airport about an hour ago. Ruby needed to see you immediately."

Cole paused and waited for Ruby to elaborate. But she just sat in her chair, smiling warmly but distantly, as if she had just finished off a bottle of wine by herself. Her hair was several inches longer now and, surprisingly, she was sporting a makeup-free face. He cast a confused glance over to his father, but Arthur was suddenly very interested in a speck on the table.

"I'm sorry. I don't mean to be rude, but...who are you?" Cole asked.

The tall man stood up and extended his hand. "Jaxon Mulgrave, Ruby's fiancé. Very pleased to meet you." He spoke with a commanding British accent and looked to be in his mid-thirties. He wore blue tailored pants, and a matching ornate jacket. His posture was rigid and perfect, giving Cole the impression that he might be a soldier or an officer of some kind. Circular sunglasses rested on top of dark hair that had been cut into a Caesar cut.

"Hi Jackson, I'm --"

"No. It's *Jaxon*. With an 'x.' No 'cks.' I always know when someone says it the other way." He gave a twisted smile, sat down again, and put his arm around Ruby.

"Um. OK. Well, I'm Cole. Di-Did you just say that you're her fiancé? When did that happen?!"

"I was curious about that myself," Arthur said, a slight edge to his voice. "Oh, and sorry about the lack of food. I didn't realize that we would be having guests tonight." He moved over to the refrigerator to start preparing dinner.

"It happened yesterday. Ruby was very adamant about getting back to Mechanica City as soon as possible. She couldn't wait to tell you about the good news. Isn't that right, dear?" Jaxon turned to her and Ruby smiled and nodded.

"Well, that's...that's great news. Congratulations," Cole answered halfheartedly, his mind spinning. He felt unsteady and taken aback, like he had missed a step going down a staircase. This was all moving extremely fast, even for Ruby. She was known for making impulsive decisions, but *marriage*? He never thought that she would rush into something like that.

"How did you two meet?"

"Well, it's a...funny story," Ruby said, finally speaking. "Jaxon and I met when I came back...to L.A. after finishing the...Erika Glam tour. He waited for me outside...of the stage door...with flowers. It was so...romantic." She turned her eyes to Jaxon and uncharacteristically fluttered her eyelashes. "I knew right away...that he was the one."

Arthur returned with a plate of bruschetta and a large bottle of red wine. Cole attempted to catch his eye again, but Arthur seemed to be purposefully avoiding his gaze. Cole grabbed the bottle of wine and filled his glass to the top.

"Cheers to the new couple!" Arthur said, and everyone raised a glass and clinked them together. They looked around at each other, chuckling nervously, and an uncomfortable silence descended on the kitchen – no one seemed to know what to say.

"So...tell us a little about yourself, Jaxon," Arthur said, finally breaking the silence. "What do you do for a living?"

"Oh, this and that. I started worked for my father's company after I graduated from college."

"What sort of company does your father have?"

"Manufacturing. Automobiles. He's been in the business for years. On my own, I've dabbled in the entertainment industry. Producer on a few projects. Oh, and I know some people in banking that have helped me in my career. I like to consider myself an entrepreneur," he replied vaguely.

"He's so talented!" Ruby gushed.

"Very impressive," Cole said. He tipped his head back and swiftly drained his wine glass before reaching for the bottle again. Anything to get through this uncomfortable dinner.

Jaxon's dark eyes flashed. He stared at Cole pointedly. "*Thank you*. Ruby will be well taken care of."

"Well, I love to hear that!" Arthur quipped, trying desperately to keep the energy in the room light. "So! Ruby. We've really missed you here in Mechanica City. How is everything? Any new tours lined up?"

"No. Nothing yet. I'm...not really looking. Jaxon convinced me...not to go back to work...after my last tour. We want...to start a family soon...and you can't take care of a home...if you're working all of the time." Ruby smiled dreamily, absentmindedly pulling at a strand of her hair.

"Wow, Ruby. You've certainly made a complete 180," Cole said with a strained smile.

"She just knows what she wants," Jaxon answered. "Also, you'll be pleased to know that we've decided to settle down in Mechanica City."

"That's wonderful!" Arthur said.

"Really? But Ruby, I thought you hated it here?" Cole asked suspiciously. Ruby looked at him with a dazed expression and simply shrugged her shoulders and giggled.

"She changed her mind," Jaxon said shortly.

"Apparently," Cole answered.

The rest of the evening continued in this way. Jaxon dominated the entire conversation while Ruby continued to smile and say nothing. They ate a hastily thrown together dinner of fettuccine alfredo and breadsticks and then, after the meal was finished, Arthur and Cole walked Ruby and Jaxon to the front door.

"Well, it was nice to meet you. Congratulations again," Arthur said cheerfully.

"Yeah, congratulations," Cole said. He eyed Jaxon warily.

"It was a pleasure," Jaxon said. He placed his arm firmly around Ruby's shoulder. "Thank you for dinner. You're very kind."

"Any time!"

Jaxon nodded. "Well, we must be off. We'll be staying at the Empress Hotel for the next few days while we search for a suitable place to live. Goodnight."

As soon as Arthur closed the door, he leaned against it and let out a heavy sigh. He turned to Cole with deep concern in his eyes.

"Well...that was something."

"That's a nice way of putting it. I thought it was a disaster! Who the hell is this random British guy that Ruby is *getting married to?!*" Cole asked incredulously. "And why didn't you tell me that they were coming over?"

"I was just as surprised as you were! They showed up right before you did. I'm very worried about Ruby. Something wasn't right with that guy.

But what can we do? Ruby is an adult. We can't get involved."

"Well, I don't know about that..." Cole replied, anxious thoughts swirling through his head. Arthur twisted his moustache absentmindedly, lost in thought.

CHAPTER EIGHT

The next morning, Cole made his way down the staircase in the entrance lobby of the manor house. A busy day lay before him, for it was his twenty-third birthday.

As he moved to open the front door, Arthur came around a corner and approached him.

"It's the Birthday Boy! Where are you running off to?"

"Gabe and I are going to the dirigible race. I'm excited for dinner tonight, though! Where are we going again? Ferrous?"

"Yep, a 7:00 reservation. Hey, before you go, I wanted to give you your birthday present." Arthur dug in his coat pocket and pulled out a metal wristband. The flexible bronze folded around Cole's arm; it stopped at the elbow. A small clock was fused to the wrist.

"Wow! What is it?"

"Happy Birthday! Now, press the bolt on the underside of it."

Cole reached underneath the metal wristband, pressed a button, and his body disappeared.

"What the hell?!"

Arthur clapped his hands together and laughed. "I call it the Invisibility Vambrace! What do you think?"

Cole yanked off the wristband in shock and his body reappeared. "H-How did you make this?"

"I used some of those orange crystals that we found in the Mesozoic Era."

"But I thought we didn't have any more of that stuff..."

"Well, I went and got more..."

"Dad!"

"I grabbed a small amount!"

"I thought we talked about this. You can't just go traveling through time, messing with things that -- "

Arthur's face darkened. "Come on, Cole. Am I not allowed to create things for my own son?"

"That's not what I said --"

"I'm an inventor. That's what I do! This is getting ridiculous. I'm perfectly sane and responsible. Let's not fight on your birthday, OK?"

Cole was ready to argue his point further, but he swallowed his words and let it go.

"Well...thanks Dad. I appreciate it. I'll see you later." He put the Invisibility Vambrace in his messenger bag, gave Arthur a quick hug, and then left the manor house.

Fifteen minutes later, he stood outside of Nautique, his frozen breath hanging in front of his face like white smoke. A frigid breeze blew down the busy streets and the sky hung low like a light gray ceiling. He shivered and rubbed his hands together.

Nautique's front entrance porthole suddenly opened and Gabe stepped out. He walked over and wrapped his arms around Cole. "Happy Birthday handsome," he whispered in his ear. A pleasant heat filled Cole's chest.

"Thanks! Are you ready to go?"

"Absolutely!"

They held hands and made their way down the sidewalk in the direction of the Alabaster Stadium. It was the day of the highly anticipated Race for a Cure, the annual charity dirigible race in Mechanica City that took place every first Saturday in February. The money that was raised from the race went to Lyme Every Mountain, an organization that raised money to fight Lyme Disease. Cole loved the race and made it a point to try and go every year.

As they moved deeper into the city, a crowd began to form around them. Citizens of all ages were talking excitedly, large smiles stretched across their faces. Up ahead, in between a row of silver luxury apartment buildings, the stadium finally appeared. The impressive stone edifice, with its golden domed roof and streaks of silver running along the walls, took up three city blocks.

Excitement washed over Cole as he scanned the stadium's windows and saw that nearly every seat was filled – it was going to be a great race. He and Gabe followed the boisterous crowd through the check-in point, had their tickets scanned, and made their way inside.

The Alabaster Stadium teemed with noisy and intoxicated spectators that were all cloaked in heavy coats and scarves. The smattering of different voices colliding in the air was almost deafening. Cole noticed that many people in the crowd were double fisting colorful, hand drawn posters and large draughts of frothing beer. Most of the posters were singing the praises of Jamila Masoud, the race's most recognized participant. She had won the top prize, the Aurum Cup, for the past five years in a row. Every other dirigible racer wanted to end her winning streak but, so far, no one had been successful.

Cole and Gabe wound their way through the crowded and echoing stadium, absorbing the mind-boggling sights and smells. They passed by a long row of vendor display stands where cheerful men and women sold savory food that crackled inside metal serving trays. All of it was very greasy, very unhealthy, and, most importantly, very delicious; Cole's stomach grumbled in response. Gabe bought them each a pitcher of beer and a hot dog slathered in toppings, and they ascended the steep stairs to find their seats. The race was set to start in five minutes.

As they made their way up to the top of the stadium, Cole looked down at the race track, a wide and circular dirt path that twisted and turned perilously. A circular patch of grass lay at the center of the track. Two holographic lines marked the start and finish lines.

When the sun's rays managed to break through the grey clouds, they bounced and reflected off a long row of colorful and intricate dirigibles hovering in the air along the starting line. An exposed engine sitting inside a bright red dirigible popped and growled. The golden airship next to it was encased in thick layers of sheet metal that was dotted with long, sharp spikes. Bold numbers were printed on the sides of each dirigible.

"There she is!" Gabe cried as they settled into their seats. Jamila Masoud had just walked onto the track to carefully inspect her emerald green airship for any imperfections. She ran her hands along the hood and adjusted the mirrors.

"By the way, you're never going to believe this. Guess who I saw yesterday?" Cole asked.

"Who? It wasn't your dad's girlfriend, was it?" Gabe asked.

"No, it was Ruby! She's moving back to Mechanica City!"

"What?! When did this happen?"

"She told me last night," Cole answered. "That's not even the crazy part. She's moving back because she's getting married to some random guy named Jaxon."

Gabe choked on his beer in response. "*Married?!* Th-That doesn't sound very Ruby-like. Who is this Jaxon guy?"

"No idea," Cole responded, thumping Gabe on the back. "He seemed like he comes from money, but that's really all I know. Details were pretty vague. He gave off such a weird vibe. There was something strange going on with Ruby, too. She wasn't acting like herself."

"Well, love can do that sometimes." Gabe smiled and squeezed Cole's hand.

"Yeah, I guess that's true," Cole replied. His face flushed a deep shade of crimson. "But this felt different. She acted like she was stoned or something."

"Maybe they celebrated before they came over?" Gabe wondered.

"And then I invited her to join us today, but did she answer my text? No!"

Suddenly, a loud bell rang out, echoing through the stadium – the race was about to begin!

"Ladies and gentlemen!" said a deep, booming voice that reached every spectator in Alabaster Stadium. "Welcome to the 35th Annual Race for a Cure! This is Chester Bingleton, your favorite radio broadcaster from WTKV-MC! The excitement in the stadium today is palpable. I love it! Are all of our racers ready?"

The dirigible drivers stepped into their airships and revved the engines loudly, causing the massive audience to jump to their feet and cheer enthusiastically. A mechanical woman wearing a tight dress sauntered onto the track, a red smile on her lips and a bright handkerchief in her hand. She paused at the starting line and the crowd held its breath. Then, she raised her hands high and brought them down again. The airships zoomed past her -- the race had begun!

The dirigible racers steered their airships wildly down the long and winding path, slamming into each other to try and force one another off the track. Chunks of broken metal littered the dirt. A silver dirigible came right up behind the ruby red dirigible, a shark stalking its prey, and bumped the back of it. The red dirigible wobbled but remained steady.

Next, the driver of the silver dirigible pressed a button on their dashboard and 7-foot-long spikes unfolded out of the airship hood. With a sharp tearing sound, a spike pierced the back of the red dirigible and tore off the rear engine. The red airship spun out, shuddering and vibrating, before crashing spectacularly onto the ground. The crowd groaned as the driver was violently thrown through the front window and landed in a heap in the dirt. He struggled to his feet and slammed his helmet angrily onto the ground.

"Go go go!" Cole screamed along with the crowd as the race continued. Clouds of dust rose in the air as the dirigibles sped along the race track. The green dirigible darted in between the other racers, its engine whirring loudly. It narrowly avoided smashing into them and eventually pushed its way to the front of the line. Jamila's proficiency and skill with her dirigible was awe-inspiring. She navigated her way smoothly past the tight corners of the track and sped onward, moving miles ahead of the rest of the drivers.

"Release the explosions!"
Chester Bingleton's voice bellowed throughout the stadium. Metal racks that held dozens of small black bombs suddenly rose up through the race track and were launched into the air. Fiery orange and red explosions immediately began to pop off one by one. Most of the racers flipped and drove their dirigibles out of the way, but a few weren't so lucky. Two of the racers, one in the silver dirigible and the other in a bronze one, slammed right into a stack of bombs and exploded, thinning out the competition. The crowd roared their approval.

Hastily turning her steering wheel all the way to the left, Jamila Masoud was narrowly able to avoid a bomb that went off right in front of her. However, the shockwaves from the blast sent her spinning and, with a loud popping sound, her front right tire exploded.

"In a *stunning* turn of events, Ms. Masoud has fallen back!" Chester Bingleton cried. "It appears that she is attempting to change a blown tire. The clock is ticking – will she be able to make up for the time that she's lost?"

Cole's heart dropped as a groan of disappointment rippled through the stadium. Everyone could see that Jamila was struggling – she had stepped out of her airship and was pushing frantically on a button that rested on the side of the dirigible, just above the blown tire. She pushed once, twice, three times – nothing.

"I think I'm gonna barf!" Gabe cried.

Finally, after one last push, the deflated tire popped off by itself. A long metal arm rolled out, accordion-like, grabbed a new tire, and placed it onto the hub. She jumped back into the front seat, leaned on the throttle, and tore back down the race track.

"We've now made it to the final lap and Christopher Mapplethorpe is in the lead! Will anyone be able to overtake him?" Chester declared.

Emboldened by this announcement, Jamila leaned on the throttle and sped up, quickly closing the gap between herself and Christopher. She ducked her head as three bombs narrowly passed overhead and continued driving. The two dirigibles made whistling sounds as they shot down the track, neck and neck, smashing and bumping into each other.

Cole clenched Gabe's arm and screamed, "GOOOO!!!!!"

Both dirigibles were quickly approaching the finish line. The spectators were screaming at the top of their lungs. At the last second, Jamila steered her airship into the air, flew over the top of

Christopher's airship, performed a barrel roll over a tall stack of bombs, and streaked across the finish line.

A congratulatory trumpet blast rang out and mounds of brightly colored confetti rained down onto the stadium audience. Cole and Gabe cheered and hugged each other, nearly overturning their beers in their excitement. Jamila Masoud took a well-deserved victory lap as the stadium vibrated from the cheers and revelry.

"That was one of the best races that I've ever seen here!" Cole gushed fifteen minutes later as he and Gabe made their way down one of the stadium's many staircases and walked past the vendor booths. "The way Jamila leaped over that stack of bombs?"

"I really thought that she was going to crash!"

"Amazing. She is untouchable! I can't believe Ruby missed it! Oh, did you want to stay for any of the after parties? If we're lucky, we might be able to get a picture with Jamila." A group of drunken men ran by whooping and cheering.

"I'd love to, but I still need to get a few things for your birthday dinner tonight. Do you mind if we stop by my abuela's place before I take you home? I brought over some empanadas the other day and I need to grab my serving tray," Gabe said. His grandmother had recently moved into an apartment building just a few blocks away from Cole's father's house.

"Sure!" Cole replied, and they headed down the sidewalk.

When they finally approached the quaint apartment building on the corner of a quiet street, Gabe unlocked the front door and they walked inside. They entered a cozy entrance lobby and then took the stairs up two flights before knocking on the door to 3A.

"Abuela? It's Gabe! Cole is with me. Can we come in?" Gabe asked. They waited for several seconds. There was no response.

"Abuela?" he repeated.

More silence. A few more seconds passed before he pulled out his key and unlocked the door.

They slowly made their way into the small living room. A plain floral couch, a wooden china cabinet, and a television were the only things that occupied the space. All the lights were on. Water from the kitchen faucet was running steadily into the sink.

"Abuela?" Gabe called out.

"Maybe she's taking a nap?" Cole asked anxiously.

"No. She wouldn't forget to turn off the sink," Gabe replied. His voice shook slightly.

The two boys walked further into the apartment, moving slowly through the living room and past the rest of the kitchen. They paused at the start of a short, carpeted hallway. A light was on in the bathroom at the end of the hall.

"Abuela? Are you there?" Gabe whispered.

More silence.

"Should we call someo--?" Cole asked.

Gabe ignored him and marched forward, Cole at his heels, and wrenched open the bathroom door. Both of their eyes fell on the figure of an elderly woman sprawled on the floor. Her eyes were closed and her mouth was hanging slightly open. Her face looked sickly and pale and her forehead was bleeding.

"Abuela!" Gabe yelled.

CHAPTER NINE

Cole stared at the white tile floor of the sterile hospital room and sighed wearily. His vision was blurry and his stomach grumbled loudly; it had been several hours since he had eaten that hot dog at the stadium.

He was seated in a chair that was next to a hospital bed, and its current occupant was Gabe's grandmother Camila. Long tubes and wires snaked out of her thin arms and into a large stack of square, metal monitors that stood guard next to her bed and recorded her heart rate and blood pressure.

He yawned and stretched his tired limbs – it had been a long night. His eyes passed over Camila's frail body. She was still unconscious.

After discovering her on her bathroom floor, Gabe called 911 in a panic and a blaring ambulance rushed them to the nearest emergency room, McQueen Hospital.

For Cole, it felt like time had abruptly ground to a halt and everything was moving in slow motion. As soon as they arrived at the hospital, a handful of doctors and nurses surrounded Camila and hurried her off to an operating room. Cole and Gabe were left to sit in the waiting room, dazed and rattled, for several hours.

Cole pulled out his phone to check the time – it was three o'clock in the morning. He rubbed his tired eyes and sagged in his seat. His gaze fell across a small collection of framed photographs that covered the top of a side table next to the hospital bed; Gabe had brought a large stack with him, knowing that they would be a source of comfort for Camila. Cole's eyes lingered on a black-and-white picture of a young boy with a sly smirk on his face who was seated next to a stern female companion. She held a long rifle in her hands.

"Any idea how to get through tonight?" he asked the photograph. The boy and teen girl stared silently back at him.

A soft knock at the door made him jump in his seat. The door opened and Gabe, along with an older man wearing a long white coat, entered the room. Gabe's face was drawn and pale, and dark circles hung under his eyes.

"Any news?" Cole asked anxiously, standing up quickly. "What happened to her?"

"Ms. Perez experienced a hemorrhagic stroke," the doctor explained. He wearily took off his glasses and cleaned them before continuing. "A blood vessel burst and began to bleed into her brain."

"Will she be alright?"

"It's still too soon to tell, unfortunately. We will need to monitor her and see if she wakes up from her coma. She has a long road ahead of her. Why don't you both go home and get some rest? It's late. You can come back and see her tomorrow."

Uncertainty flashed across Gabe's strained face. How could he possibly leave her? Cole's chest burned painfully -- he wasn't used to seeing him like this.

Gabe looked down at Camila and sighed deeply. "I-I guess you're right," he finally said. "I need to sleep. I'll...I'll come back first thing tomorrow."

He moved to the hospital bed and gently held his grandmother's hand. "Te amo, abuela," he whispered softly. Then he and Cole walked out of the room and left the hospital.

The moon hung high in the night sky like a glowing orb and bathed the silent streets of Mechanica City in soft, yellow light. There were hardly any cars driving along the streets at that hour which gave the city a feeling of quiet abandonment.

The two boys eventually stopped in front of the entrance gate to the manor house. They stood there silently for a minute, too exhausted to speak. The past twenty-four hours had felt like a surreal dream.

"I'm so sorry," Cole finally said. He wrapped his arms around Gabe and held him tightly, breathing in his cologne.

"No, I'm sorry. Your birthday dinner was ruined."

"Stop, don't say that. Are you going to be okay tonight? Do you want me to stay with you?"

"I'll be okay. I'm just...I'm just going to go back home an-and sleep before going back to the hospital in the morning. Oh, man...I have so much to do. Maybe I'll cook some rice and beans for her? She usually likes it when I make that. Or maybe I should make that lobster bisque recipe that she loves? I have so much to do...oh, and I-I also need to bring her a...a change of clothes..."

Without any warning, Gabe sank to the ground and planted himself on the curb, his face in his hands. Loud sobs wracked his exhausted body.

Cole rushed over and sat next to him. It felt like sharp, twisted spikes were sprouting and tearing through his intestines. It was physically painful seeing his boyfriend so fragile and distraught. Gabe was always the one that remained calm in stressful situations -- he never fell apart.

Cole gently placed his hands on either side of Gabe's face, looking him squarely in the eyes. "We *will* get through this, okay? I promise you that. There's no other option because we'll do whatever it takes."

Gabe continued to cry for several more seconds, but eventually he wiped his eyes and slowly stood up again. "You...You're right. Sorry for blubbering, this is a lot to deal with. I love you."

"No need to apologize. I love you, too. Get some sleep and I'll talk to you tomorrow."

They kissed deeply and then Gabe slowly made his way back to his apartment. Cole watched him leave, feeling more anxious and uncertain than he had allowed Gabe to see.

*****

Camila was here, and then, like a candle being extinguished, she was gone. There was nothing that anyone could have done, which is what the doctor said to Gabe, but this did little to ease his overwhelming grief. For Cole, the next several days were a blur of phone calls, long nights spent with Gabe, and helping to organize funeral arrangements. He didn't have the mental bandwidth for much else.

On a gray Tuesday afternoon, Camila was laid to rest in a plot at the center of Glaisher Cemetery, which was positioned at the back of Camila's beloved parish, St. Rotwang Catholic Church. Gabe's entire extended family, all his various aunts and uncles and cousins, showed up for the funeral to pay their respects. They brought overwhelming amounts of delicious food, heaps of colorful flowers, and their beautiful memories of Camila's life. They instantly embraced Cole as one of the family, and despite the sadness and solemnity of the occasion, Cole didn't want to be anywhere else.

Two long and arduous weeks passed by, but better times finally arrived on a bitterly cold Friday night in February. Cole, along with Brody and Safi, stood on the curb in front of the Empress Hotel. It was the night of the Senior Ball and they were all feeling buoyant with excitement as they stood and shivered in their most formal attire: Cole's slim-fit, black tuxedo had a classic silhouette with sharp lines; Safi was clad in a long black tunic, or *thawb*, with white embellishments on the collar and sleeves; Brody had dyed his hair aquamarine and had stuck sparkling pins and brightly-colored buttons onto the lapel of his gray tuxedo. As always, he was looking to make an impression.

"Is Gabe on his way?" Safi asked impatiently, his breath rising in the cold air. He rubbed his arms up and down in a futile attempt to stay warm.

Cole pulled out his cell phone for the umpteenth time and checked for any new text messages. Suddenly, a square icon blossomed onto the front of the glass screen -- a message from Gabe.

BE THERE IN ONE SECOND!

Exactly one second later, Gabe appeared from around a corner and jogged over to them. He was also dressed in his very best, with a tailored white jacket over black dress pants and shiny black shoes. A small plastic box wrapped in a bow was tucked under his arm, and a toothy white smile lit up his face. Cole thought he looked amazing.

"Sorry I'm late! I was held up at work and then the cable car was packed and took forever." He kissed Cole on the cheek and looked around at the rest of them with excitement in his eyes.

"Hey, Gabe! It's great to see you. I'm so sorry about your grandmother," Brody said sympathetically.

"Thanks Brody. I really appreciate that," Gabe replied. "Oh, I almost forgot! Cole, this is for you." He pulled a colorful boutonniere out of the plastic box and pinned it to Cole's lapel.

"Hey! You didn't get *me* a boutonniere!" Safi cried. Brody's face paled and he threw Gabe a look that seemed to say, "Thanks a lot."

"Umm yes, that may be true...*but* I did bring a little something for us to enjoy before we go in!" He hastily pulled out a small bottle of whiskey that was concealed in his jacket pocket and passed it around. They each took several long swigs of the warm liquid and, when they were all feeling properly buzzed, they turned around and strode through the front doors and into the hotel.

The main lobby was just as vast and awe-inspiring as Cole remembered it, having last been there two years before while on his first date with Gabe. A massive crystal chandelier hung from the center of the ceiling, its many layered branches of bright prisms bathing the tiled floor below in warm, effervescent light.

Hundreds of Cole's senior classmates, each of them wearing high collared tuxedos or long formal dresses with bustles that stuck out at the back, walked by him. A dozen well-dressed mechanical hotel employees were greeting and directing people towards a ballroom off the main lobby.

As soon as Cole, Brody, Safi, and Gabe stepped into the ballroom, their eyes bulged in shock and awe. The large, circular space that they had stepped into was an East Asian fantasy, as if the entire country of Japan had suddenly sprung to life in the middle of the hotel.

Every year, one of the dozens of different cultural appreciation clubs at Brume University was chosen to decorate the Senior Ball. Last year, the Indian Cultural Club was in charge of decorating and they had somehow managed to fly in two massive elephants that students were able to take pictures with.

The Japanese Cultural Club was determined to create something truly magical this year, and they had overwhelmingly succeeded: several large ice sculptures of Japanese landmarks like the Itsukushima Shrine and the Osaka Castle, each one several feet tall, stood next to circular tables; a large stage covered by a canopy of pink cherry blossom branches from Kyoto held a cover band of the 1960's rock group The Golden Cups that sang and strummed on their guitars; a dance floor had been placed in the center of the ballroom where packs of students moved and swayed to the music.

"It looks amazing in here!" Brody gushed. "Wow, they really pulled it off. Oh, did you guys want to get our rings?"

Everyone nodded in agreement. They moved through the crowded space and walked over to a long row of tables that were fronted by lines of students. A member of the Japanese Cultural Club kept each table organized.

Each year, senior students would receive a ring that commemorated their status as seniors and, to some students, their entire university experience. The rings were a Brume University tradition.

After they had finished making their way through the long lines and finally picked up their rings, Cole, Brody, Safi, and Gabe paused at a nearby table to admire their shining loot. Brody had chosen a silver band that was embedded with a sapphire and had a quote from his favorite play *As If He Hears* running along the inside of the ring, while Cole's ring held a ruby gem in the center and the math formula $M = Fd$ along the band.

"OK, enough of this! It's time to dance. Are you ready, Safi?" Brody asked, and without waiting for an answer, he grabbed Safi's hand and dragged him away.

"That sounds like a great idea," Cole said, but before he could leave the table, Gabe grabbed his hand and held him back.

"Can I talk to you for a second?" An anxious expression rested on his face.

"OK. Sure," Cole answered, and Gabe led him over to a different table.

"Are you OK? What did you want to talk about?"

Gabe nervously grabbed Cole's hands and stared deeply into his eyes. "Well, I-I've been thinking about this for a while. The past three months, actually. And, um, I'm nervous to ask you this, as you can see. But I'm also excited!"

Cole chuckled and waited for Gabe to gather his thoughts. *How did he get so drunk already?*

"So...we've been dating for about two years now. My longest relationship."

"Mine too!"

"And we've had so much fun together! I feel so happy when I'm with you."

Cole, his stomach fluttering pleasantly, squeezed Gabe's hands. "I feel so happy when I'm with you, too."

"You've supported me through my lowest points. My first few months at Nautique. And now with...with my abuela. I couldn't have gotten through it without you. You've also *literally* saved my life!"

Cole chuckled. "And I would do it again. I'm starting to get nervous, though! What did you want to ask me?"

Gabe took a deep breath and said, "Will you move in with me?"

The wide smile that stretched across Cole's face suddenly cracked and fell off, like a cliffside crumbling into the sea. This announcement was very unexpected – they had never even discussed this casually!

"I...I...I..." he stammered. His forehead broke out into a nervous sweat and he struggled to formulate words.

"So? What do you say?" Gabe asked.

Move in with you? Already? Cole had never lived with a boyfriend before. What if, after a few months, they got sick of each other and their relationship disintegrated? What if Cole found a great job in another city? An endless list of negative and irrational scenarios flashed quickly in his mind.

"You don't seem happy."

"No! No, that's not it at all! I'm just, uh, processing," Cole responded. His thoughts felt scattered and slow, like a sputtering computer struggling to wake up. *What the hell is wrong with you? Say something!*

"It's just...things have been going so well between us. You're going to graduate in a few months. I don't know, this just seemed like the perfect time to ask," Gabe said dejectedly.

"It's not that. I-I'm being stupid. It's just...what about my dad, you know? He isn't fully recovered from his time in the Mesozoic Era. I'm also not sure if I can trust him around *The Astrolabe* anymore--"

"But he has a girlfriend now, right?" Gabe asked. "Not to mention all of the work that he's doing at Bennett Industries. He seems to be doing much better!"

"It's just...Yeah. I...I guess you're right..." Cole gave a perfunctory nod of the head, yet he couldn't shake the feeling that things in his life, once again, were moving too fast. A surge of anxiety bloomed in his chest that took his breath away. He had, perhaps naively, assumed that there was still plenty of time left before they would start

talking about something like this. However, Gabe
was staring at him, waiting for an answer, so Cole
shoved a strained smile on his face and laced
his fingers with Gabe's.

"Can I take some time to think about it? Is
that okay?"

A pained expression rolled across Gabe's
face, but it disappeared just as quickly as it
appeared.

"Of course. Take all the time that you need!
I love you," he replied, gently squeezing Cole's
hand.

"I love you too."

"Well, are you still in the mood to dance?
Let's go!" Gabe said, and the two boys hurried over
to the dance floor.

The energy inside of the ballroom was
buoyant and joyful as the senior class danced and
swayed to the thumping music coming out of the
speakers. Everyone in the crowd was smiling and
moving around the dance floor, drinking in the
moment and the heightened atmosphere. But not
Cole. He felt a deep chasm of nostalgia cracking
open within himself, getting bigger as the minutes
slipped by. He blinked back bittersweet tears while
dancing close to Gabe under the swirling lights. If
only he could freeze this moment and repeat it over
and over again. Everything in his life seemed to be
changing. His time at Brume University was
speeding to an end and there was nothing he could
do to stop it.

An hour later, the music suddenly died down
and a bespectacled young man wearing a crooked
smile on his face approached the microphone stand
on the wooden stage. The nametag on his chest read
President of Student Affairs.

"Good evening, Class of '30! How are we all doing tonight?" he asked with a squeaky voice. Everyone in the room cheered in response.

"Excellent! Now, the moment that you've all been waiting for has finally arrived -- the crowning of the King and Queen of the Senior Ball!" A strained silence fell over the audience as everyone anxiously awaited the results. The President of Student Affairs slowly pulled out an envelope from the inside of his jacket and paused for dramatic effect.

"The Senior Ball Queen is...can I get a drum roll, please?"

The drummer with the cover band hurriedly beat a steady rhythm on one of his drums.

"The Queen of the Senior Ball...for the class of 2030...is...*BIANCA CHESWICK!*"

The room broke out into muted, polite applause, yet Cole couldn't help but roll his eyes. Bianca strutted through the audience like a preening peacock with a large smirk on her face, her large black sequin gown trailing behind her, and strutted her way up to the stage where she collected a diamond tiara from the President of Student Affairs. He reverently placed it on top of her head and another small smattering of applause rang out. Cole rolled his eyes again.

"And now...our King of the Senior Ball is...*BERNARD ADEBAYO!*"

A spotlight swiveled over and locked onto a dark-skinned boy with his mouth hanging open in shock. His thick dreadlocks were piled high on top of his head and he was dressed in a silver tuxedo. This time, the crowd erupted with raucous cheers and applause, Cole cheering the loudest, and Bernard rushed to the stage. Bianca scowled at getting a much cooler reception from the audience than Bernard received, but she kept quiet while he accepted his crown.

Three hours later, long after most of the students had left the ball to head to after parties, Cole and Gabe stumbled out of the hotel in a daze and stopped by the curb to wait for Brody and Safi. Cole took a deep breath of the night air and sighed pleasantly.

"Where do you think they are? I haven't seen them all night," Gabe asked. "Brody missed seeing Bernard get crowned!"

"I don't know! Maybe they're --"

"YOU ARE SUCH A BASTARD, BRODY!"

Safi suddenly burst through the hotel's main entrance, his face flushed with anger. He stormed by Cole and Gabe and made his way down the street, cursing the whole time. Brody ran after him.

"WAIT! SAFI, COME BA--! Oh, hey guys!" he said, skidding to a halt. He looked like he wanted to disappear into the floor. "Um. S-Sorry about this! Safi and I are, uh, having a moment."

"Is everything okay? Where have you been?" Cole asked.

"The bar. We've been fighting pretty much all night. I'll tell you about it later. I have to go chase after him. SAFI, WAIT!" And he ran down the street after his boyfriend, gasping for breath and clutching the stitch in his side.

CHAPTER TEN

Thin, powdery snow began to fall as Cole and Brody walked inside the coffee shop. It was the day after the Senior Ball, and the two boys had decided to meet up at Crema in Figgenbottom to discuss the weekend's events over coffee and pastries. Crema, where Cole had worked as a barista two years before, sat inside a dusty shopping center.

They spotted an empty table next to a window and put their things down.

"I'll get our drinks," Cole said, and he made his way past a series of mismatched tables and approached the main bar. A beefy, dark-skinned man with kind eyes was wiping off a porcelain mug.

"Hey Pendleton! How's it going?"

"Back again? This is the sixth time this week!"

"OK, listen. You're lucky that it's not twice a day," Cole replied with a laugh. "What can I say? This is where my caffeine addiction started! Oh, I've been meaning to ask you – how are things here now that JP is finally gone?" JP, or Jean Pierre, Malbec was the former co-owner of Crema. He was a lazy and vain man with greasy hair who possessed near-constant sour breath and enjoyed bullying Cole. After his husband James Holloway III, the other co-owner, discovered that JP was cheating on him, their marriage dissolved and, eventually, they got divorced. Pendleton took over as the new co-owner.

"Man, listen...you know that I don't like talking about former employers, but...can I be honest with you?"

"Of course!" Cole answered eagerly.

"Things are perfect! Never better. Last week, JP screamed at Mr. Holloway, so Mr. H finally had him clear out his office. That drunk mess went and caused a scene in front of the customers! I'm so glad he's gone. By the way, you have to remind me to tell you about the new lady I'm dating. I'm telling you, man – I think she's The One."

"Can't wait to hear all about it," Cole replied, feigning enthusiasm. Pendleton had a curious habit of falling deeply in love with any woman that showed even the slightest bit of interest in him. He was perpetually lovesick.

Pendleton made two lattes and then Cole made his way back over to Brody.

"Ugh thanks. I really need this today," Brody moaned as Cole passed him his drink. He slowly massaged his temples.

"I somehow managed not to drink that much," Cole said. "Anyway, what happened last night? Safi looked pissed."

Brody grimaced and sipped his drink. "Girl...what a night. Hot mess. OK, so Safi and I stopped dancing and jumped in the line for the bathroom. We were both pretty drunk at this point. Everything was fine while we waited in line. Totally normal. And then I got a phone call from my agent."

"Wait. You have an agent? When did this happen?"

A self-satisfied smile stretched across Brody's face and he nodded excitedly. "Last week! Sorry that I forgot to tell you, things have been hectic. My acting professor introduced me to this amazing man named Alan Saperstein who is based in New York City. He's been in the business for forever and he really knows his stuff."

"Congratulations, Brody!"

"Thanks. But yeah, so, I got a call from Alan right as the Crowning Ceremony started, so I told Safi to give me a second and that I would meet him back on the dance floor. I mean, I only needed, like, five minutes. But Safi didn't like that. He *freaked out* and started screaming at me. He called me a liar and said that I'm too much of a coward to break up with him."

"Yikessss," Cole said sympathetically. He did not envy his best friend in that moment. "Can you clarify something for me? Did you and Safi actually have plans together after graduation? Something about a theater company? I just don't understand why he's so angry all the time now. It's not like him."

Remorse flickered across Brody's face and he blushed deeply. "Well...I may have said that I wanted to start a company with him..."

"Brody!"

He groaned. "I know, I know! I just sort of said it one day, but I wasn't being serious. It sounded like a good idea at the time!"

"You are the worst," Cole chastised. "Would that actually be so bad, though? Staying here with Safi to start that theater company? We could all pretend to be adults together!"

Brody let out a sigh and shook his head. "It's too late for that. Safi broke up with me last night."

"What?!"

"Yeah. He said that I didn't pay attention to him. I only care about my career. You know, maybe this was inevitable."

"Inevitable? Why would you say that?"

"It's true!" Brody replied, his eyes filling with tears. "Guys have always thought that I was weird. And then I finally get a boyfriend, and what do I do? I screw it up. Maybe I should just admit to myself that I'm a self-absorbed narcissist."

"Don't say that, Brody! That's not true, that's just Safi talking. So, you're passionate about your career. Is that a bad thing? How does that make you selfish? Safi is a nice guy, but what he said is complete crap. Besides, having a boyfriend isn't the most important thing in the world. You'll be OK."

"Easy for you to say," Brody mumbled.

Cole chuckled. "I'm serious. Don't think that you're broken because you've had bad luck in the relationship department. It will happen again! You're going to find someone who won't make you feel bad about being ambitious."

Brody slowly nodded in agreement. "Thanks Cole. You're right – things will be OK. If I'm honest with myself, things between us weren't great for a while. Safi just went ahead and made the decision for me. At least I don't have to feel bad about moving to New York now. I can't believe I used to want a boyfriend so badly. Oh God, remember when I used to have a crush on you?"

Cole laughed and blushed. "Yes, I do."

"I'm *so* glad that we never screwed things up by dating. You couldn't handle all of *this*, anyway."

Cole laughed again. "I'm going to miss you when you go to New York. Can everything please stop changing? Like, slow down a bit. I can't keep up!"

"I don't know, I think it's kind of exciting. Emotionally draining, yes, but also exciting. Imagining what the rest of this world has to offer. So many of my classmates are sad to leave Brume, but I'm ready. I've never been anywhere, other than Seoul for family reunions. I want to take everything in while I'm still young enough to enjoy it! New York City feels like the perfect place to start."

Cole leaned back in his chair and drained his mug, ruminating over everything that Brody had said. Even though his stomach felt like it was melting into a puddle of pure gloom, he kept an upbeat expression propped up on his face.

"Well, try not to forget about all of us after you leave!"

"But things will be changing for you, too! It's not like you're getting left behind or anything. Your problem is that you're too indecisive. And uptight."

"OK I get it."

"And a little timid."

"I said that I get it!"

"By the way, how is your job search going? Have you applied anywhere new?"

"I sent in an application to this relatively new startup company called Gossamer. I haven't heard anything back yet. Ugh. It gives me anxiety when I think about it."

"Wow. This conversation is heavy," Brody laughed. "Subject change – how is Gabe? Did he have fun at the Senior Ball?"

"He did. I have to tell you, though, that I had some boy troubles of my own last night..."

"What happened?"

"Well...Gabe asked me to move in with him."

Brody choked on his latte and sputtered, "H-He did what?!"

Cole launched into the story of last night's emotional conversation with Gabe, and Brody listened intently, rapt with attention, his mouth hanging open comically.

"Wow, Cole! I mean, *wow*. That is, like, a major life decision. What did you tell him?"

"Well...nothing. Nothing really. I asked for some time to think about it."

"Think about it? Are you crazy?! You've only been dating for two years!" Brody exclaimed. "You're ready to live together?"

Cole groaned. "I don't know! What's wrong with me? I know that I love him. Very clear on that. But sharing an apartment...like you said, are we ready for that? I'm not sure. To be honest, I'm not really sure of anything at the moment. There's just too much going on right now to even think straight."

"Hmm...well, I'm no relationship expert. Obviously. But one thing I do know is that once you sign that lease, you're locked in for a year. Take your time to think about it," Brody said earnestly. Cole nodded in agreement.

"Well, on that note, we better get to class." The two boys returned their mugs to the main bar, gathered their things, and walked out of the coffee shop.

*****

Later that night, Cole made his way through the frigid cold metropolis to meet up with Karma. Earlier that morning, she had called and asked him to join her at a bookstore called Bruckerman's for a meeting of NAAM. Tonight was the final planning meeting for the upcoming March for a Change, Mechanica City's very first march for mechanical civil rights. Cole didn't really see himself as a political person and didn't know what to expect, but it had been several weeks since he had last seen Karma and he wanted to support her. Arthur was having dinner with his girlfriend that night, too, so Cole was thankful for any excuse to stay away from the manor house.

It was an uncomfortable thought, but Cole had to admit to himself that Mechanica City was really struggling these days. Incredibly, no new information concerning Project Hominum had been discovered and no arrests had been made. Stories of mechanicals getting attacked and mugged filled the nightly news reports. Cole couldn't explain it, but he could sense a very palpable aura of paranoia and anxiety hanging over the city like a storm cloud. He could see it in the faces of the strangers that passed him on the sidewalk, hardened expressions that seemed to say, "Get me the hell out of here." He shivered and pulled his heavy jacket tighter around him.

As he was walking by a post office, his phone suddenly vibrated in his pocket, so he paused underneath a nearby green awning and pulled it out. A text message from Karma was waiting for him:

I NEED YOUR HELP! I can't make it to the meeting tonight because I fell down the stairs in my apartment. I'm such an idiot! On my way to St. Stewart's right now to get my ankle replaced. Would you mind taking notes for me? I hate to miss this meeting. Text you later!

A wave of disappointment crashed over Cole and he sighed with irritation. *Now I have to go by myself?* He wouldn't know a single person at this meeting. Unhappy with that dreary prospect, he briefly considered turning around to go back home, but a mental image of an injured Karma spending the night in the hospital stopped him in his tracks. Why was he angry? It's not like Karma planned on spraining her ankle. Besides, he *did* come all this way, after all, so he ducked out from underneath the green awning and continued walking towards Bruckerman's. He promised himself that he would check on Karma tomorrow at her apartment.

Five minutes later, the dusty bookstore appeared up ahead. Cole felt momentarily nostalgic because he used to work here for a short time. He looked down at his wristwatch – ten minutes to spare. He walked towards a heated patio outside of a French bistro and sat down at an empty table. Neon blue light from an LED advertising screen across the street fell across Cole's table, glowing brightly in the cold night. Every few seconds, the advertising screen would change and a new product would be displayed. A familiar face suddenly appeared on the screen, catching Cole's eye –The Great Roderigo! His rugged and handsome face, along with his signature moustache, stood out clearly against the glowing ad space. He had a new studio album dropping next month. Cole chuckled, suddenly recalling a chaotic memory from two years ago: a crowded concert hall, blaring music, and the sound of Ruby's screams as The Great Roderigo was flung around a stage by his ankle. As thoughts of Ruby popped into his head, his stomach filled with anxiety. He hadn't talked to her in weeks.

Cole checked his watch again. With five minutes left before the meeting, he decided to give his sister a call. He pulled out his phone again, selected her image in his contact list, and pressed the Video Chat button. A dial tone rang for several seconds before a viewing screen popped up. It showed the shabby floor of a room.

"Ruby? Are you there?" he asked. There was a loud shuffling sound from off camera and then the camera view shifted and, finally, righted itself. Ruby's pale face stared out at Cole. She was sitting alone inside a dark bedroom; heavy drapes had been dragged across the windows, blocking any light from coming in. Her glazed and unfocused eyes were puffy and red, as if they'd been rubbed raw, and a faint black bruise spread across her jaw.

"H-Hello Cole," she mumbled sluggishly, the lids of her eyes drooping heavily. "What...do you want?"

Cole's eyes bulged and he reeled back in shock. *What the hell, Ruby?* What happened to your face?"

"What do you mean?" she asked shakily.

"The *giant bruise on your face, Ruby!* What happened?!"

"Oh, th-this? I fell. I was cleaning the apartment and... I tripped. I'm clumsy." She giggled inexplicably and then massaged her jaw.

Cole stared at her suspiciously. "Are you sure? No offense, but you're acting weird."

Ruby nodded her head but wouldn't meet Cole's gaze. "I-I'm fine. I swear. Why are you calling? Do you...need something?"

Cole's stomach churned uncomfortably. Something wasn't right. Ruby looked visibly uncomfortable. "Well...I just wanted to check on you. Catch up. I mean, we haven't talked since you moved back. You missed the dirigible race!"

"Sorry. I've...I've been busy."

"What have you been up to?"

Ruby giggled again and stared into space.

"OK...well...where's Jaxon?"

"I-I think he's at work or something."

"You *think* he's at work? You don't know?"

Ruby fell into a heavy silence, one full of tension and stifled words. She nervously pulled at a loose strand of hair.

A streak of white hot anger suddenly whipped across Cole's mind and he lost his temper. "RUBY! Tell me what's wrong! I don't know why you're lying to me."

"I...I..." A muted *bang* came from behind her and her eyes grew wide. She was looking at something off-camera.

"What was that?" Cole asked, panic rising in his throat.

"I-I have to go, Cole. Don't tell Dad about this, OK?" Her pale face disappeared as the screen went black.

"Ruby! Wait!" Cole yelled. With a dense feeling of dread filling his chest, he selected her image again in his contact list and waited. And waited. And waited some more – she didn't pick up.

He slammed his fist on the table in frustration and put his head in his hands, agonizing over what his next move would be. Ruby was in trouble, he was sure of it, and he was determined to help her. But why did she want him to hide this from their dad? Nothing was making any sense. He felt a pang of guilt about missing the NAAM meeting, but he pushed it away – Ruby was in danger. Karma would understand. Cole turned around and ran down the sidewalk away from Bruckerman's, cutting a straight path toward Ruby and Jaxon's apartment. Luckily it was only a few blocks away.

Ten minutes later, he finally reached the block that they lived on and came to an abrupt stop. *This can't be right*, he thought, but after double checking the address that Ruby had texted him months before, he realized that he was in the correct location. A line of ramshackle grey apartment buildings with dark, shrunken windows lined the empty street, a long procession of dreariness. Everything was eerily quiet. Ahead of him, Cole spotted a disheveled mechanical man slumped over on the curb.

"H-Hey kid, y'got some oil? I could really use some," he slurred aggressively. Cole shook his head and continued walking.

Near the end of the block, he slowly approached an apartment with a peeling red door and a rusty door knocker. 1601 -- he was at the right place.

How does Ruby live here? He thought, scrunching his nose at the smell of trash that hung heavily in the air. He could see a light inside the apartment, the only source of light on the entire block. Ruby or Jaxon must be inside.

"RUBY! RUBY, IT'S COLE! COME TO THE WINDOW!" he shouted, cupping his hands around his mouth. He waited on the sidewalk and stared up at the window, blood pumping in his ears, desperately hoping that Ruby would answer his calls.

Suddenly, a dark shadow passed in front of the window.

"JAXON, IS THAT YOU? WHAT DID YOU DO TO RUBY, YOU BASTARD? YOU BETTER LET HER--"

The rest of his sentence stuck in his throat as he was blasted off his feet and thrown roughly to the ground. He sat up slowly in a daze, ears ringing, and stared ahead of him in horror. A massive orange fireball was rising in the distance, a monstrous explosion, staining the dark sky with a jagged flash of bright light.

Cole didn't know how he knew it, but a terrible realization suddenly overwhelmed him – Bruckerman's was on fire!

CHAPTER ELEVEN

Cole struggled to his feet and, with no thought for his safety, he ran towards the scene of the explosion. Sweat poured down his face as he raced down the street, through dark alleyways and past ever-increasing amounts of terrified people, until he turned a corner and skidded to a halt in front of Bruckerman's. The roof of the bookstore had collapsed and a gaping, jagged hole had taken its place. Long, orange flames moved through the wreckage and clawed at the air, casting a fiery orange glow across the surrounding city blocks.

Massive slabs of cracked cement and charred beams of wood littered the street in front of the bookstore. Men and women covered in black dust and ash stood in groups and stared at the destruction in muted horror, unable to process what they were seeing. Cole swayed where he stood as he looked around at the carnage, hoping that someone would walk out unscathed. The bookstore had been standing only moments before...

"WATCH OUT!" someone screamed.

Cole's eyes grew wide and, at the last second, he jumped out of the way as a flame-covered wooden beam teetered on its edge and then slammed onto the street. Crowds of people scattered in all directions.

A soft humming noise filled the air, growing louder and louder, and an icy chill crawled down Cole's spine as he looked up and saw the now familiar circular aircraft hovering above him. It was silent and menacing, a metal predator staring hungrily at its prey. With a groaning sound, a metal hatch slid open on the underbelly of the airship and a pile of white sheets of paper were dumped into the air. They fell slowly through the air and blanketed the street below, bouncing off the heads of the gawking crowd. With trembling hands, Cole slowly bent down and picked up a sheet of paper from off the street. It read:

CITIZENS OF MECHANICA CITY!
Were our instructions difficult to understand?
Did we not make our demands clear? The events
of tonight should change that. Robots are NOT
in charge of this city anymore.
Project Hominum sees everything. Think about
us the next time that you want to organize a
march for filthy robots. Anyone who is allied
with the disgusting metal creatures will suffer
when this is all over. We are everywhere and we
are always prepared.
Prepare for more. *They will not replace us!*
#HumansFirst

There was a deep grumbling sound. The fractured walls of the bookstore wobbled from side to side before crumbling spectacularly to the ground; a large cloud of dust bloomed out of the wreckage. Cole realized that he needed to leave before he was seriously injured, so, with one last look at what was left of Bruckerman's, he turned around and ran back to the manor house.

The following morning, the streets that surrounded Bruckerman's had been blocked off with long rolls of neon yellow caution tape and gruff police officers closely monitored who came in and out. Cole turned on the news and watched as hulking, red firetrucks aimed their hoses at the smoldering wreckage, still attempting to put out the blaze.

Mayor Simpson held an emergency press conference in an attempt to calm the citizens of Mechanica City and ease the tensions that had erupted overnight. With an air of unshakeable authority, he announced that he was reinstating the Mechanica Protection Agency, a special task force that investigated and neutralized domestic terrorist activity. Hordes of police officers, some from outside of the city, swarmed the downtown area and were instructed to rifle through bags and interrogate anyone who looked suspicious. The city was officially on lockdown. A week-long curfew was swiftly put into effect, but this did little to ease Cole's anxiety; Project Hominum could strike at any time, day or night.

Brume University canceled classes for the day, so Cole unexpectedly found himself with no plans, but he was thankful for this because it was imperative that he speak to Karma as soon as possible. Arthur balked at this idea, but after assuring him that he would stay alert and safe while he was out, Cole left the house and made his way to Karma's place of employment. NAAM was situated at the lowest point in Mechanica City, so he was forced to use the cable car to reach it. During the hour-long commute, Cole spent the time feverishly typing out text messages to Ruby, begging her to call him. She never responded.

The cable car eventually pulled to a stop in front of a cluster of hunched, sagging office buildings that stood in front of a large cemetery. Cole walked through the front door and into a stale, white waiting area. Cheap furniture and a chipped, wooden receptionist desk were all that filled the small room. Hanging from the walls were colorful posters that said, "Mechanical Rights Are Civil Rights!" and "Have You Been the Victim of a Hate Crime? Here Is a List of Organizations That Will Help You..."

Cole approached the receptionist desk and a mechanical woman waved him through into the next room, which was an open office space lined with rows of identical cubicles. The sounds of clacking keyboard keys and tense, hushed voices filled the room. Each cubicle was occupied by a mechanical man or woman answering phone calls or shuffling through papers. Cole passed by a mechanical woman saying into a headset, "NAAM will *absolutely* be continuing our work, despite the terrorist attack! We are committed to --"

Karma stepped out of a doorway up ahead. She was leaning on a pair of crutches with a grim expression on her pale, silicone face. With a wave, she ushered Cole into her office.

The room had a low ceiling and was very cramped; only a cheap wooden desk and two folding chairs could fit comfortably inside. Karma hobbled over to the desk, which was covered in stacks of disorganized papers, and Cole sat in the chair across from her. It creaked as he sat down.

"So...how are you feeling?" he asked.

"Oh, this?" she said, looking down at her ankle. It was wrapped tightly in gauze. "This is nothing, I'll survive. My doctor said that I can take the gauze off in a week. But what about you?! How are *you* feeling? Cole, I can't tell you how happy I am that you're sitting in front of me right now. I was sick with worry last night. There was a moment, as I was sitting in the hospital bed, when I thought...when I really thought that you might've been killed when that bomb went off."

There was a brief, strained silence. Karma sighed and wiped her eyes.

"What the hell is going on, Karma?" Cole finally whispered.

"Well, I think it's clear that mechanicals are no longer safe in this city. Every day I wake up with this ominous feeling in my stomach that never leaves," she replied morosely. "Something worse is coming, I know it. And we need to be ready. I naively assumed that after two years the fringe voices of dissent surrounding mechanicals would have disappeared, but that's...obviously not the case."

"How did Project Hominum find out about the meeting? It doesn't make sense. Do you...do you think someone inside the group told them?"

"Well, we didn't exactly make it a secret," she replied. "Flyers were hung up and we advertised for it online. But it couldn't have been an NAAM member. They would never do something like that."

Cole nodded but remained unconvinced, so he kept his thoughts to himself. They lapsed into another strained silence.

"All of those people...my *friends*. Charles and Grace and Svetlana. So many more. They're all dead. Everyone inside of Bruckerman's was incinerated," Karma finally said, staring into space. "They were all there because of me."

Her chin wobbled and then the floodgates opened – tears poured down her face and she began to sob. Cole moved around the desk and put his arm around her shoulder.

"Karma, don't blame yourself. You didn't bomb Bruckerman's. A bunch of disgusting pigs did it."

"I know, but I asked them to go there --"

"But how could you have known what would happen? That's impossible. This wasn't your fault."

Karma sniffled and slowly nodded her head. "I...I guess you're right..."

"Now, I wanted to talk to you about something." He sat back down in his chair and looked at her intensely. "I know that I've said this before, but --"

Karma cut him off with a wave of her hand. Her eyes glowed brightly and a blotchy red hue bloomed on her cheeks. "Don't start with that, Cole."

"I'm being serious. Can't you just pause the activism for a bit? Just to be safe? I mean, people were murdered, Karma! You were almost one of them! I don't want you to get hurt."

"*No,* Cole," she replied. "I can't do that. No, I *won't* do that. That would be giving Project Hominum exactly what they want!"

"But --"

"You have to understand that they don't want us to be vocal. They want mechanicals to shut up and disappear."

"I just don't want anything bad to happen to you."

"I know, but I can't even think about myself right now. This is bigger than me, Cole. The NAAM is not going to stop. In fact, we're going to be more vocal than ever! I mean, think about it – could we have defeated Malick if we had ignored him and hoped for the best?"

Cole let out a deep sigh and sat back in his chair, feeling frustrated and deflated. Why was she fighting him on this? He was just looking out for her. And yet, she presented a fair question. Ignoring the issue of Malick would have created a space where he could have taken over Mechanica City faster and with more damage. Was he focusing on the wrong thing?

"I...I guess you're right. I mean, the NAAM can't just lay down and do nothing. I'm just worried about you, okay? But, with that said, I'll still help you in any way that I can."

"Thank you, Cole. I really appreciate you saying that. The NAAM is going to be working extra hard to ensure that the police are actually doing their jobs and that the bastards who did this will be located and held accountable."

"Do you think the MCPD could provide you with some security at least? Maybe a cop patrolling outside your apartment or something?"

"It's possible. I'll reach out to them and see if I can pull a few strings. I've done them a few favors in the past. By the way, the surviving members of the NAAM and I are planning a vigil tonight for everyone that was killed in the blast. You should come."

"Where are you doing it?"

"It took a while to decide, but we ended up choosing Bruckerman's. It'll send a powerful message if we go back there."

With no warning, painful images from the previous night's harrowing events suddenly flashed before Cole's eyes; terrified strangers running and screaming in the streets, the acrid smell of smoke burning his lungs. His forehead broke out into a heavy sweat and he started feeling lightheaded.

"Um. I...B-Bruckerman's? I'm sorry, Karma, but...um, I'm sorry. I-I don't think --"

"Are you OK?"

"It sounds stupid, but I-I can't go back there yet."

Now it was Karma's turn to look concerned. "That's not stupid, Cole. Don't worry about it, I completely understand. You can always come to the next meeting."

An hour later, Cole hugged Karma, left her office, and headed back to the manor house. While he was on the phone with Gabe, recounting the events from last night, a text message from Arthur popped up on his screen:

Hey son, I have a question: Sabina wants to have dinner at the house tonight. With everything going on in the city, she didn't want to be alone. I'd love for you to finally meet her. What do you think? Does 6:30 sound good?

Cole came to an abrupt stop on the sidewalk. "Gabe? Let me call you back," he said, and he sat down on a nearby wooden bench to think. His stomach sank miserably. *Does 6:30 sound good?* No, it didn't sound good at all. On top of everything that was going on, this was the last thing that Cole needed. In case Sabina hadn't noticed, there was a terrorist attack last night. There could be another one any day now. Not only that, but he still needed to think of a way to tell Arthur about the situation with Ruby.

But at the same time, he *had* promised Arthur that he would be supportive...even if it killed him. So, he begrudgingly picked up his phone and responded to his father with a short and simple message:

Fine.

*****

That night, just before six-thirty, Cole slowly shrugged on a dinner jacket, splashed water on his face, and then flew down to the manor house from his apartment airship. An uncomfortable layer of irritability hung over him as he made his way down to the kitchen; he was anxious for a drink. *Let's get this over with.*

As soon as he opened the kitchen door, a blast of steam struck him in the face and obscured his vision. Through the haze, Cole could see Arthur rushing around the room like a frenzied ball of energy. He hastily chopped romaine lettuce with one hand while the other hand sautéed a pan of roasted chicken. A large pot of water boiled on the stove.

"Hey, Dad. What are you making?"

131

"Cole! Glad you're here!" Arthur replied. A large and toothy grin was plastered on his face, causing his grey moustache to curl up at the ends. "We're having garlic butter chicken with potatoes and a Caesar salad. Would you mind chopping up some parsley and thyme? Sabina said this was her favorite, but I've never made it before and I want to make a good impression." He went back to bustling around the kitchen and mumbling to himself, so Cole poured himself a big glass of wine and reluctantly prepared to chop some herbs.

Ten minutes later, a sound like tinkling wind chimes came from the main lobby – the front doorbell. Arthur looked up in shock.

"Sh-She's early! Umm OK. Uh. Wh-What should I do?"

Cole couldn't help but laugh. "Maybe you should answer the door?"

"Oh. Yes! Right." He nodded and scurried out of the kitchen. Moments later, he returned with a visibly nervous Sabina in tow. She slowly walked through the doors, smiling demurely. Cole was finally able to get a good look at her; she was wearing a long, navy blue dress that fell to her ankles and her long black hair had been pulled back and styled attractively.

"Cole, this is Sabina. Sabina, this is Cole," Arthur said, beaming.

"Nice to see you again," Cole muttered. His immediate impression was that she seemed nice enough, but he wasn't ready to lower his guard just yet.

"You too. Apologies for not introducing myself the other day. I was just shocked to see you fall out of the sky!" She laughed lightly and nervously pulled at the clasp on her purse.

132

A few seconds of awkward silence passed between them as they looked at each other, unsure of what to say or do next. Cole chugged the rest of his wine and then moved to refill his glass.

"Why don't I show you what Cole and I have been putting together for dinner? Care for some wine?" Arthur asked, and, with his hand hovering over her lower back, he led her carefully around the kitchen.

While they talked and observed the crackling food, Cole sat down at the kitchen table and silently observed Sabina, feeling apprehensive. What if he couldn't think of anything to say to her? Or worse, what if she turned out to be a terrible person and he was forced to grit his teeth through the entire evening? His stomach churned uncomfortably, so he attempted to quiet it down with more wine.

A timer next to the stove ticked by softly until, five minutes later, it released a loud *ding* – the food was ready. Cole and Arthur finished setting the table, and they sat down to eat. The effects of his wine had finally set in, and Cole was feeling buzzed and emboldened; why shouldn't he embrace this unexpected opportunity? He could finally grill Sabina and find out what her true intentions were with his father.

"So...how did you two meet?"

"We met at work, actually. Sabina came to Bennett Industries to interview me for *The Daily Pastiche*, remember? It was for that article about those jetpack cannisters that we built for the police department."

"Oh, right."

"I didn't want to do the stupid interview, since I hate talking to the press, but Sabina here made me feel very comfortable." He chuckled and softly stroked the top of her hand. Cole averted his eyes and stared down at his plate. *Don't say anything. Don't say anything...*

"So. Anyway," he said, changing the subject. "What do you do for a living, Sabina? You interview people, is that right?"

"That's right. I'm a general assignment reporter for *The Daily Pastiche*," she answered pleasantly. "I cover a range of stories that happen in Mechanica City, anything from human interest to organized crime."

So, you get paid to get information on people... Cole thought.

"I worked in the newsroom for many years as a producer, but six months ago I was finally promoted. Now, instead of working in a basement, I work on the thirtieth floor!"

"I'm sure you've seen her on the news, Cole. She's very talented," Arthur gushed. He turned to look at Sabina again, beams of infatuation shooting out of his eyes. A stronger wave of white-hot irritation suddenly rolled over Cole, threatening to overwhelm him. How much of this ridiculous display would he have to endure? His father was acting like a lovesick teenager. Images of his mother bubbled up to the front of his mind and a lump formed in his throat. Using every ounce of his energy, he willed himself to shove his feelings away.

"I don't really watch the news, but I'm sure you're fine. Do you make good money?"

Sabina smiled apprehensively. "I, um, I make enough."

Arthur flashed his eyes angrily, but Cole ignored it. He had a nice buzz going on now and saying exactly what was on his mind felt good.

More awkward silence passed.

"Have you ever been married before?" Cole asked pointedly.

Sabina blushed deeply. "Um, yes. Twice before, actually."

Twice before? That's not a good sign.

"Wow. Twice, huh? Couldn't make it stick?"

"Cole!" Arthur shouted in protest. "Stop it."

"What? I'm just asking questions," he argued back. He turned to Sabina and said, "Look, I'll be honest with you: you seem like a nice person, but I just don't get your intenti --"

"Enough!" Arthur barked, slamming his hand on the table. A tense hush fell over the kitchen. "You're being extremely rude to my guest. If you can't act like an adult, you should leave."

A loud snort suddenly came from the end of the table. Cole and Arthur abruptly stopped arguing and turned to look at Sabina in shock. Her eyes were closed and she was chortling into her hands.

"Wh-What's so funny?" Arthur asked, laughing in spite of himself. Cole wondered whether she had lost her mind.

"I'm sorry!" she finally said, wiping tears from her eyes. "I don't mean to laugh, but this conversation is hilarious!"

"What do you mean?" Cole asked.

"Well, it's just that I'm used to being the one that asks all the tough questions. I've almost forgotten what it's like to be on the receiving end! Have you ever considered a career in journalism?"

"Um, well. I --" Cole spluttered.

"Now, to answer your
very *pointed* questions, no I wasn't able to 'make
them stick.' I had a habit of marrying emotionally
stunted men who liked to spend all our money."

"You don't have to talk about this," Arthur
said.

"No, it's OK. Most people react the same
way when I mention my past marriages. I'm used to
it. Anyway, I've worked on myself and now I'm in
a much healthier headspace. Oh, and in case you
were also wondering, I don't regret my past
decisions. I believe that everything happens for a
reason." She said all of this very matter-of-factly
and took a satisfied sip of her wine.

Cole reeled back in shock, suddenly feeling
like he had been struck in the face. The buoyant
wine buzz that he had coursing through him
disappeared like a candle being snuffed out, and it
was replaced by a prickly and uncomfortable feeling
of shame. *How the hell do I respond to* that? he
thought. Sabina was much more perceptive than he
had expected, picking up on his subtle digs the way
that she did. Like a water balloon getting popped,
his suspicion and anger poured out of him. He felt
foolish.

"I...I don't know what to say..."

"I suggest you apologize," Arthur said, but
Sabina held up her hand and he fell silent again.

"That's not necessary. Cole is just being
protective. I can't blame him. I did the same thing
with my stepfather when we first met."

"You did?" Cole asked in surprise.

"Sure! I didn't want some strange man
talking to my mother! But it all worked out. He and
my mother will celebrate their thirtieth wedding
anniversary this year. Anyway, I want you to know

that my intentions with your father are entirely pure. I simply want to get to know you and Arthur better. I'm not trying to become a replacement for anyone."

Cole looked at her curiously. *Who is this woman?* he wondered.

"So! Now that we've settled that...I noticed that airship floating above the house," Sabina said, skillfully changing the subject. "It's very impressive. Who built it?"

"Oh right, I forgot to tell you!" Arthur answered. "Cole and I built it together over the summer."

"That's fantastic!" Sabina replied. Her bright and warm smile eased any remaining tension that was in the air. "Arthur told me that you're in the aeronautic department at Brume University. You know, even though I work in a completely unrelated field, I've always been interested in aeronautics."

"Really? You like airships?" Cole asked in surprise.

"Oh yes! Part of my job as a general assignment reporter is to be curious, so I get to investigate and become knowledgeable about a wide range of subjects. Speaking of which...now is probably a good time to ask you something."

"What is it?"

"Arthur told me that you witnessed the explosion at Bruckerman's last night."

Cole glanced at Arthur nervously, but his father nodded encouragingly.

"I-I did. I was heading there for a, um, meeting when it blew up."

Sabina's brown eyes grew wide in shock. "Oh my goodness, that's awful. I'm so happy that you weren't injured. Would you mind if I interviewed you? The paper is asking me to write an article about the terrorist attack, and I'm looking for eyewitness accounts. Nothing too invasive, just some questions about what you saw and experienced. Details are still pretty scarce right now and you would be an excellent source."

"Oh! Um. Well, I appreciate the offer but I'm not sure. Can I remain anonymous? To be honest, I was, um, heading to a NAAM meeting that night, and I'm nervous to make that information public."

"Not a problem at all, I completely understand. You can absolutely be an anonymous source."

"I'd be happy to tell you what I saw then. Did you want to do it now, or...?"

"Oh no, let's do it tomorrow. We can meet up for coffee or something!"

"Excellent! It's all settled then," Arthur said cheerfully. He beamed at Cole and Sabina. Cole noticed that Arthur's hand hadn't shaken at all throughout dinner.

Thirty minutes later, Cole collected their empty plates, put them in the sink, and then they walked Sabina to the front door.

"That was such a nice dinner," Sabina said. "I can't thank you enough."

"It was our pleasure," Arthur answered. He pulled Sabina into his arms and they hugged tightly for several seconds. This time, Cole couldn't think of a single snarky comment.

Sabina broke away from Arthur, turned to Cole, and said, "It was great to finally meet you. Thank you for making me feel so welcome."

Cole swallowed a sharp sting of remorse and muttered, "I'm really sorry about earlier..."

"Don't worry about it," she said. "No hard feelings."

"Wait until you meet my daughter Ruby!" Arthur said. "She's a ball of energy. By the way Cole, have you heard from her lately? She isn't responding to my text messages. I invited her tonight."

At the sound of Ruby's name, Cole's stomach immediately went cold; he had somehow completely forgotten about her over the course of dinner.

"Actually, I've been meaning to talk to you about tha--"

A high-pitched whistle suddenly blared throughout the house. Large red emergency lights emerged from the walls and started spinning and flashing.

"What is that?!" Sabina yelled, covering her ears with her hands to block out the shrieking alarm.

"*THE ASTROLABE!*" Arthur screamed. He ran over to the closest wall, made a series of tapping movements, and then stood back as a small screen and keypad slid out of the wall. As soon as the keyboard was in position, he feverishly typed out a series of codes that scrolled across the screen.

"What's going on?" Cole asked.

"What's *The Astrolabe?*" Sabina asked.

Cole stared at his father, panic rising in his chest, and waited for him to offer an explanation. *Why the hell is he talking about The Astrolabe in front of Sabina?*

"One second, please!" Arthur shouted, still frantically typing in codes.

"No, tell us now! What is happening?" Cole shouted back, raising his voice over the deafening noise. The alarm was starting to make his ears throb.

"FINE! That alarm you're hearing? It means that someone has broken into – Aha! Here we go!" The blaring alarm abruptly shut off, and a booming silence fell over everything. Cole massaged his aching ears.

"What the..?" Arthur stood back and stared, open-mouthed, at the small screen on the wall; Cole and Sabina ran over to look. Black-and-white security camera footage was displayed on the screen. Arthur pressed a key and the camera slowly zoomed in on his vast laboratory. A chaotic scene was unfolding inside: a jagged, gaping hole had been blown out of one of the laboratory windows and a small band of masked strangers were crawling inside, shards of glass littering the floor. Their masks were shiny and gold, with gears for the eyes and circular air filters covering the mouth. Everyone was wearing a mask. Everyone except for...

"Ruby!" Cole shouted.

Two of the masked intruders gripped her roughly by her shoulders and pushed her through the broken window and into the laboratory. She was blindfolded and gagged. The intruders made their way to the floating white door and stopped in front of it.

"Oh no..." Arthur groaned.

A tall and broad-shouldered intruder walked to a cupboard, shot the lock off, and took a spare pocket watch. Then, they pointed it straight at the giant glowing white door and it opened slowly with a groan. The group of masked strangers cheered in celebration and hurried through the door; three of them stayed behind. Suddenly, the broad-shouldered intruder turned around and looked straight at the security camera; a chill went down Cole's spine. The stranger reached up and pulled their mask off -- it was Jaxon.

CHAPTER TWELVE

"What is he doing?!" Cole cried out in anguish.

With a venomous sneer, Jaxon reached into his coat pocket, pulled out a large sheet of paper, unfolded it, and held it up to the security camera. The note read, "Follow us and she dies." He turned and ran through the white door.

"Um...could someone please explain to me what is going on?" Sabina asked. "Is everything OK?"

"No. Everything is definitely not OK," Arthur answered grimly. "My daughter has been kidnapped by her fiancé."

"You're not making any sense, Arthur. And what *is The Astrolabe?* Is it a computer program or something?" She stared at them expectantly, brows furrowed in confusion. Cole and Arthur looked at each other for a moment, a sharp coil of anxiety passing silently between them. Revealing the truth about *The Astrolabe* would certainly create unexpected complications. Could they trust her? How would she handle the news? Not only that, but revealing the truth would almost assuredly change the very nature of Arthur and Sabina's relationship. Would they be able to survive it? There were so many unknowns to navigate and no time to do it. A decision had to be made now.

"Should we tell her?" Cole finally asked after a moment of silence.

"We don't have much of a choice at this point," Arthur replied uneasily. "Sabina? I, um, need to explain something to you. How do I say this? You see, *The Astrolabe* is, um....it's..."

"*The Astrolabe* is a train that can travel through time," Cole finished for him.

Sabina stared at them for a moment, eyes wide in bewilderment, before she threw her head back and released a boisterous laugh, the sound like the tinkle of piano keys. But when neither Cole nor Arthur joined her in her laughter, choosing instead to simply stare at her in silence, her face dropped, and she fell silent.

"Y-You're serious?"

"Deadly serious," Arthur replied.

"A time traveling train? Don't be ridiculous, that's impossible."

"It is very much possible."

"I...I need to sit down." Sabina's face paled and she started to sink to the floor. Arthur ran to her and pulled up a chair.

"I'm sorry, darling. I really wanted to tell you -- it's true! But President Carver swore me to secrecy after we saved the city from Malick."

"President Carver asked you to lie?!" Sabina cried.

"It's a bit of a complicated situation. I'll explain later. Anyway, she made me promise to keep *The Astrolabe* a secret or else the government would confiscate it," he explained. "But I *was* planning on telling you. At some point..."

"Y-You're saying that the government knows about this?" Sabina said. She pulled out a paper fan from inside her purse and waved it in front of her face. "For how long?!"

"About two years," Cole answered.

Sabina fell silent. She stared at the floor in a daze, visibly struggling to process this bombshell. Nothing was making any sense. But a few moments later, with a stiff shake of her head, she sat up straighter in her chair and collected herself.

"My apologies. This is a lot to take in."

"I'm sorry that you had to find out like this," Arthur said mournfully.

"No, don't be sorry. I completely understand why you kept this a secret. It should stay a secret! I can't believe that you really created a time machine. How marvelous! You're amazing."

A large grin spread across Arthur's lined face and his cheeks burned bright red. "Well...I, um, I had a lot of free time..."

"Those strange intruders...where do you think they're going in *The Astrolabe?*" Sabina wondered.

"I haven't the slightest idea, I'm afraid. They could be going anywhere. The implications of changing anything in time are disastrous, so we need to hurry," Arthur said. "How could Jaxon even know about the train? Ruby knows that it's supposed to stay a secret."

"Oh, she definitely knows," Cole said firmly. "I don't think she willingly gave that information up. Jaxon forced her to tell him somehow. I mean, I talked to her yesterday and she had a black eye!"

"What did you just say? *A black eye?!*" Arthur raged. "*Why didn't you tell me this?!*"

"I'm sorry! I wanted to tell you, but Ruby made me promise not to say anything." Cole leaned against the wall and put his face in his hands. "Dammit! I...I didn't do anything to help her!"

Arthur stopped pacing angrily around the room. He walked over to Cole and put his hand on his shoulder. "Hey, don't say that, son. It's not your fault, you thought you were doing the right thing. I mean, if anyone should be blamed, it's me. I'm the dad. I should've been paying more attention. And I'm...I'm sorry for making the spare pocket watches. You were right to be worried. But we're not going to give up, right? We'll think of a way to fix this."

"So...what do we do now?" Sabina asked.

Before anyone could answer, the sound of heavy footfalls began to fill the room. The blood went out of Cole's face as he turned to look at the door leading to the laboratory. Someone was quickly approaching.

"I forgot about the remaining intruders..." he whispered.

"What do we do, Arthur?" Sabina groaned.

"Follow me!" Arthur shouted, and he ran to the opposite end of the main hall, Cole and Sabina in tow. He stood in front of a wall, made a horizontal wiping motion with his hands, and a large metal door materialized.

The door to the laboratory suddenly burst open and three armed guards ran inside. Their eyes fell on Arthur, Sabina, and Cole and they smiled ruthlessly.

"Get in!" Arthur yelled, and Cole and Sabina ran through the door. Right as Arthur pulled the door shut, the armed guards slammed into it. They screamed and pounded their fists on the door.

"Are we safe?" Cole asked anxiously.

"For the moment, anyway," Arthur answered. "This panic room is pretty impenetrable."

Cole looked around at their surroundings. They were standing in a dark room, not much bigger than a large closet, and the walls and floor were made of slabs of thick steel. Rows of security cameras ran along one wall and looked down on each room in the manor house. Cole could see the intruders standing just outside of the panic room.

"What do we do now?" Sabina asked.

"I might have an idea," Cole answered. A plan was slowly forming in his head. "It's a place to start, at least. Last night, before the explosion went off, I stopped by Ruby and Jaxon's apartment. A light was on, but no one would let me in. There must be a reason for that. If I can sneak into Jaxon and Ruby's apartment and look around for clues, maybe I can find something that will tell us where they're going and why."

"How can I help?" Sabina asked.

"You don't have to do anything. I'm just sorry that you got dragged into this," Arthur answered.

"Don't be ridiculous! I want to help. How about this: why don't I go back to my office at *The Daily Pastiche* and start researching this Jaxon guy? I have a few contacts that might be able to help me dig up information on him. Where he's from, where he's worked, etc."

"That's a great idea," Arthur said. "We can find out information much faster that way."

"We'll have to find a way to get past those guards, though," Cole said.

"Do you still have the Invisibility Vambrace?" Arthur asked.

"It's in the spare bedroom. Why?"

"Take it with you when you go to Ruby's apartment. It will keep you safe in case there's any trouble."

"But how do I get past the guards outside?"

"Leave it to me," Arthur said. He held his wristwatch to his mouth and whispered the words, "Activate Blitzkrieg Mode."

"What is 'Blitzkrieg Mode?'" Sabina asked.

"Just watch."

They moved over to the security cameras and waited. They could see the intruders talking to each other in the middle of the hall.

"Any second now..."

At the corner of one of the security cameras, Cole suddenly noticed Sprocket entering the main hall. The silver cat paused in front of the staircase and stared at the group of intruders. They stopped talking and turned to look. One of the intruders moved towards the cat, hand outstretched, and then it happened – like a shiny, silver hurricane, Sprocket jumped in the air and ripped off the intruder's mask. With a swipe of her sharp claws, she furiously ravaged their face and knocked them, screaming, to the ground. Deep, red gashes were carved into their cheeks.

"SHOOT IT!" an intruder screamed. But despite their large guns, the other intruders were no match for the robotic feline. Sprocket jumped from intruder to intruder, claws outstretched, taking each one out until they were all lying on the ground and groaning in pain. Sprocket jumped back to the floor, licked her paw, and slunk out of the room.

"Now's your chance, Cole! Meet us in front of *The Daily Pastiche* building. Make sure that you take Brody or Gabe with you!" Arthur said.

Cole shoved the panic room door open, moved quickly past the intruders squirming on the floor, and ran up the staircase. His feet pounded against the carpeted floor as he ran down a hallway, turned left, and kept sprinting. His focus had narrowed and the only thing he could think about was the bronze wristband.

Two minutes later, he burst through the door of the spare bedroom and skidded to a halt. His heart was pounding painfully in his chest, but he ignored it and threw open a closet door. The Invisibility Vambrace was sitting exactly where Cole had left it. With no time to lose, he picked it up and laid it on his left wrist, where it tightened on its own; the experience was still very unnerving. Cole took a deep breath, tried to center himself as best as he could, and sprinted down the stairs and ran out of the manor house.

A heavy feeling of dread hung over Cole as he made his way down the dark city streets. He knew that the odds of a bomb going off were very low, but he was anxious nonetheless. His paranoid thoughts propelled him forward.

By the time that Cole came upon the line of scummy apartment buildings, Brody was already waiting out front.

"What's going on? Your text sounded frantic. Oh, and by the way? It's freezing out here!" Brody said. He was bouncing in place and rubbing his hands together.

"You're never going to believe this!" Cole said, and for the next few minutes he hastily brought Brody up to speed on the events of the past hour. Brody's mouth hung open in shock the entire time.

"Holy crap! Well, we definitely have to get inside. But how?" Brody asked.

"I don't know yet, but we'll figure something out," Cole answered. The two boys took a moment to observe the exterior of the apartment building, their eyes passing over the rough brick walls for any sign of a stray foothold; nothing materialized. They wound their way around the right side of the building and stood in front of the bare stretch of wall. This side had been haphazardly assembled during construction, so the wall was riddled with places to climb.

"Wait here and stand guard," Cole said. Pressing his hands to the red stone, he hoisted himself up onto the wall and slowly inched his body upwards. The process was slow going and uncomfortable. Sweat poured down his face as he gritted his teeth and continued climbing.

Ten minutes later, he had made it a third of the way up the wall.

"Brody!" he yelled, gasping for breath. "I-It's working! I'm almost th--"

With a loud shriek, Cole's hand slipped and he slammed roughly onto the ground. Brody ran over to him and helped him up.

"Are you okay?" he asked.

Cole's eyes were crossed as he stumbled to his feet. He shook his head and dusted off his pants.

"Well...I guess climbing is out of the question. But, there has to be a way to get in."

Cole and Brody tried everything: they chucked large rocks at the windows, contemplated digging a tunnel underneath the apartment, and then tried to pick the lock on the front door with a sharp tool. Nothing worked.

"That's it – I'm freezing out here," Brody said irritably. He sank down into a squat stance and leaned back.

"Wait, what are you doing?" Cole cried.

Brody jumped forward and roundhouse kicked the shadowy front door. It flew off its hinges with a loud *bang* and slammed onto the floor.

"OW! I really need to start going to Karma's classes again. My form *sucks*." He winced and massaged his foot.

"Be careful!" Cole whispered. "We're trying to be stealthy here." He looked around in a panic and held his breath, expecting a rush of armed guards to come pouring out of the doorway.

"Cole, no one is here," Brody chided, and they slowly entered the dark apartment. The living room was completely empty and the air was stale. A short flight of stairs stood at the back of the room.

"What a dump," he said. "How could anyone li--"

"Hello there." A smug woman who was holding an AR-15 in her rough hands suddenly appeared at the top of the staircase. She cocked her gun and pointed the barrel at the two boys. They threw their hands up in surrender.

"Cole..." Brody whispered anxiously.

"Tsk tsk tsk. Very naughty," the woman cooed. Her voice was high-pitched and breathy. She had a piggish face and short blonde hair. "Jaxon said that we might have some pesky intruders snooping around tonight. Didn't you know that a locked door means that you can't come in?"

Cole glared at her. "Where did Jaxon take Ruby?"

The blonde woman sneered and slowly shook her head side to side. "Can't tell you that. He wouldn't like that very much."

"You better tell me right now!" Cole barked.

The woman shook her head again, smiling widely, and then she aimed her gun and released a thunderous round of bullets into the ceiling. Brody and Cole screamed and hit the floor as debris rained down on them.

"What the hell are you doing?!" Brody bellowed.

"You're not wanted here! Leave now or I'll fill you with bullets."

Cole glowered and shook with rage, frantically considering his options. Would he be able to tackle her and rip the gun out of her hands? It was a risky choice. What if the gun went off and hit Brody?

"Fine," he growled. "But you're an idiot if you think this is over. We'll be back." He turned and marched out of the apartment, Brody following close behind.

"Prepare yourselves," the blonde woman said. Her voice followed them out of the apartment and back onto the street.

"What does *that* mean?" Brody asked.

"No idea. She's a total psyc--"

A high-pitched whistling shriek suddenly filled the air. The fast-moving noise rolled across Mechanica City and slammed into Cole and Brody, causing the inside of their skulls to vibrate.

The ground beneath them cracked and shifted violently, knocking them off their feet, and the sky began to wobble and thrum.

"What's happening?!" Brody screamed. He curled into the fetal position and covered his ears. Cole grimaced and covered his ears as well, white hot terror rushing through him like lightning. A bright flash of light exploded above them, lighting up the sky, and Cole and Brody blacked out.

*****

Holloway Prison was a silent and heavily fortified stone structure. It consisted of square, ominous watchtowers as well as many dark and interconnected corridors that were filled with the sounds of human misery.

Thin patches of trees and sloping green lawns surrounded the prison. The hazy orange sun sank slowly behind the clouds, abruptly cooling down the humid air that had persisted all day. A group of men and women that were dressed in filthy prison garb greatly appreciated the change in temperature, for they had been doing hard labor in the eastern-most courtyard all day.

One such grateful prisoner, a tall man named Oscar Wilde, stood in front of the barred window in his tiny prison cell and took deep, steadying breaths of the cool air. He struggled to keep his despair from overwhelming him as thoughts from his past plagued him for the hundredth time that day.

Oh, Bosie...my wretched, insouciant, golden love. How I loathe you and love you in equal measure...

Oscar sat down on a thick slab of stone that served as his bed and coughed violently into a stained handkerchief. An unceasing cold had kept him in near-constant pain for the past several days and he could barely make himself eat. It was difficult to imagine how his life could possibly get any worse.

There was a heavy knock at his prison cell door. Oscar jumped; there were barely any sounds in his life these days. The prison guards made sure to keep the prisoners as isolated as possible.

"Is...Is that you, Sir Edward?" Oscar asked nervously. Sir Edward Clarke was serving as his counsel during his upcoming trial.

There was no answer from the other side of the door.

"Hello?"

A broad-shouldered man that Oscar had never seen before opened the door. He was dressed in a crisp police uniform.

"They're ready for you now."

"Excuse me, but I've never seen you before," Oscar said suspiciously.

The guard stared at him for a moment. Then, he pulled out a billy club and slammed it against the cell wall. "ON YOUR FEET!" he bellowed. Oscar yelped, scrambled to his feet, and left the prison cell.

The broad-shouldered guard led him down long stone corridors that were bathed in shadows, past gloomy prison cells filled with glowering prisoners, until finally they walked out of the front doors and got into a black horse-drawn carriage. Dread filled Oscar's chest -- something felt off-kilter. None of the other guards in the prison had spoken to them as they walked out. In fact, they hadn't even looked at him. *Maybe they were just too disgusted to look at me, celebrated playwright or not,* he thought gloomily. Chalking his feelings up to pre-trial nerves, he closed his eyes and settled in for the journey.

Forty-five minutes later, the carriage slowed to a stop in front of the Old Bailey, the criminal court building in central London. The broad-shouldered guard yanked Oscar out of the carriage and shoved him towards the entrance.

"Excuse me, sir, but you are being rather rough. And why are we going through the front entrance? And where is my counsel, Sir Edward Clarke?" Oscar said. The dense feeling of dread in his chest returned with a vengeance.

"Never mind that. Keep moving!" the guard growled.

As soon as Oscar walked through the door, something strange happened -- his vision blurred and then went black. When he came to, he was standing in front of the court room.

"Wh-What happened? How did I get here?"

"They're ready for you," the guard said. Oscar could hear many muffled voices coming from behind the wooden door.

"Wait! I can't do this. I-I-"

The broad-shouldered guard put his hands on Oscar's shoulders and turned him to face him. He flashed a cold smile.

"One more thing before you go." With a roar, the guard shoved a dagger deep into Oscar's stomach. The playwright's eyes bulged in horror as thick blood began to pour from his wound. The guard kicked open the door and roughly pushed Oscar inside. Men and women that were sitting in the court room jumped to their feet and erupted into cries of shock at the sight of Oscar's bloodied body. By the time that everyone fled the room in a panic, there was no sign of the broad-shouldered guard.

CHAPTER THIRTEEN

Cole was roughly shaken awake by the sound of a rumbling explosion. It was a struggle to open his eyes. Eventually he sat up, groaned in pain, and looked to his left – Brody was sprawled out on the ground. Cole shook him awake and he sat up, eyes half-open, and looked around in a daze.

"Wh...What happened?" he asked softly.

"I don't know," Cole replied shakily. He staggered to his feet and helped Brody up. The sky above them was burnt orange and it tossed and roiled like a turgid sea. Dark plumes of black smoke rose into the air in the distance.

Stars popped in front of Cole's eyes and he pressed his hands to his temples – his head was throbbing. A thin line of blood ran out of each ear.

"Did Project Hominum attack again?" Brody asked. His breath was coming in short bursts and he was starting to panic.

"I don't know. Come on, Brody, we...we need to keep moving. Let's head to *The Daily Pastiche* and make sure that Dad and Sabina are OK. Maybe they can tell us what's going on."

Fifteen minutes later, Cole and Brody ran up the front steps of *The Daily Pastiche* building and burst through the entrance; the doors were unlocked. They ran through the dark and empty main lobby, past bright orange walls and an enclosed garden with tall birch trees, and stopped in front of a row of elevators. A sharp spike of anxiety stabbed Cole's stomach. *Where are the lobby guards and receptionists?* he wondered. The elevator doors opened and they jumped inside.

The moment that the elevator doors opened onto the thirtieth floor, the loud shriek of an alarm bell assaulted Cole and Brody's ears. They walked into a large room that had descended into chaos: dozens of men and women dressed in business casual clothing wandered around the room in a daze, blood pouring out of their nostrils, expressions of shell-shocked horror hanging off their faces.

"Something...Something is wrong. Where is Jane? JANE?!" someone screamed.

"Dad? Sabina? Where are you?" Cole called out. He tried to get someone's attention to help guide him, but no one wanted to help.

"What are we going to do?" Brody asked. "I don't see them anywhere."

Suddenly, something buzzed in Cole and Brody's pockets. They hurriedly pulled their phones out and saw a bright yellow notification on the glass screen – *The Daily Pastiche* was, amazingly, going live with an announcement. Cole tapped the notification and a video opened.

"Is it working?" a low voice whispered from off-camera.

"It's perfect. Hello, this is Sabina Greggson with *The Daily Pastiche*, reporting to you live from Rustin Avenue in downtown Mechanica City." She was standing on the corner of a busy intersection with a microphone in hand. "A series of shocking events has taken place in the city. First responders and officers with the MCPD are working quickly to restore order, but things have spiraled out of control. An hour ago, a great flash of light lit up the sky, causing widespread loss of consciousness, as well as bleeding from the --"

The sharp sound of shattering glass interrupted her – an angry mob had just tossed a wooden bench through the window of a retail store, sending shards of glass flying across the sidewalk. They cheered as they jumped through the jagged window opening and rushed into the store.

"Why is she in the middle of all of that?" Brody cried.

"Details are still coming in, but here's what we know: most, if not all, of the mechanical citizens in this city have disappeared. We don't know if the entire country has been affected or the motive behind this incident. Sources have told me that President Carver is putting together a task force that will unearth the details of what happened. In addition, the National Guard has been deployed and they will arrive in a few hours to curb the increase in property damage and looting. This is a developing story. We'll report back when we have more information." The video went black.

"Did she just say that mechanicals have disappeared? Th-That's ridiculous. What is she talking about?" Brody asked.

"I don't know. Maybe she's just mistaken. We have to find her and my dad and make sure they're safe."

"Rustin Avenue is only a few blocks away."

"And that's where Nautique is. We need to make sure that Gabe's safe, too," Cole said. It took all his energy not to start panicking. "Let's get out of here."

The streets were eerily quiet as they made their way to Rustin Avenue. Every street lamp along the way was pitch black; Cole assumed that the city's electrical grid had been damaged. The whole city was drowning in darkness.

Cole sent a text message to Gabe, asking him to meet them outside. Against all odds, Gabe responded back immediately and agreed to meet them.

Ten minutes later, they passed through a dark alleyway and came upon Rustin Avenue. The air was filled with thick smoke that burned their lungs. They walked past a row of storefronts that were overrun with looters, grabbing as many items as they could get their hands on. Traumatized men and women covered in soot and ash strolled the sidewalks, their gaze cloudy and unfocused, calling out for their missing friends and pets. A squad of police vehicles hurtled down the street, sirens blaring at full volume. It seemed to Cole and Brody that a nightmare had descended upon Mechanica City, one that they couldn't wake up from.

As they hurried past a burning flower shop, their phones buzzed in their pockets again – an update from Sabina. Another video screen appeared and they could see that she was now in front of a smoking, mutilated jewelry store. Ash covered her from head to toe, and her face was drawn and anxious.

"Welcome back. This is Sabina Greggson with *The Daily Pastiche*, reporting live from Rustin Avenue. My sources have now confirmed that every mechanical in the world has disappeared, including our very own Mayor Simpson. *Please*, whatever you do, find shelter and stay out of harm's way. Things are --" She screamed and ducked out of frame as a Molotov cocktail sailed through the air and smashed against the wall of the jewelry store.

"I repeat – get off the streets! Stay inside --"

The video suddenly cut out and faded to black. There was only silence.

"SABINA!" Cole screamed at his phone. A wave of panic nearly brought him to his knees.

"We-We're almost there! Let's keep moving!" Brody said.

They sprinted down the street until they came upon the damaged jewelry store. The area was devastated – large, jagged craters had been punched into the street, and downed power lines leaned into smashed windows. Bruised and bloodied bodies were laying on the sidewalks.

"GABBEEE! DAD? SABINAAAA!" Cole yelled, scanning through the crowds of distressed people running by him for any sign of his loved ones. He was surrounded by a blur of terrified faces.

"Cole! Collleee!" said a voice. It was faint and impossible to determine its location. Cole and

Brody looked in every direction, listening as hard as they possibly could.

"DAD? GABE?"

Suddenly, a crowd of people parted and Arthur and Sabina appeared in the distance. They could see a large, bloody gash on Sabina's forehead and Arthur's left leg was twisted and broken.

"What happened?!" Cole asked. He leaned down to help his father up, but Arthur winced in pain and sank back to the ground.

"We...We got caught in the crossfire between Project Hominum and some pro-mechanical activists," Arthur said. He was gritting his teeth in pain. "My leg..."

"We have to get him to the nearest hospital," Brody said. He helped Sabina to her feet.

"That's, like, seven blocks away, though," Cole said. "We'll never be able to make it."

"COLE! COOLLLEEEE!!!" A deep voice reverberated out of the darkness. A rush of excitement flooded through Cole.

"GABE! Over here!"

Gabe appeared among the crowd and pushed his way over to the jewelry store. He looked slightly disheveled, but he was alive. Cole ran and wrapped his arms around him.

"I'm so happy to see all of you!" Gabe said. "I had to help Dell board up Nautique so that looters don't get in. What happened? Another terrorist attack?"

"That flash of light? That was a shift in time," Arthur explained. "I've encountered them in my research. This is not good."

"The mechanicals have disappeared. All of them. We don't know much more than that yet," Sabina said.

"Wait...*all* of them? Are you sure?" Gabe asked incredulously.

"Karma won't answer my texts..." Cole replied. Hot tears burned his eyes.

"Do...Do you think the cable car is still running?" Arthur asked. The color had drained out of his face.

"I doubt it," Brody answered.

"There's a delivery dirigible sitting in a shed behind Nautique. It should seat all of us!" Gabe said.

"Are you sure that you want to go back there?" Cole asked.

"Yeah, it's not too bad. Follow me!"

A few minutes later, they approached the submarine-themed restaurant. Behind it stood a squat and dusty shed.

Gabe pulled off a white sheet and revealed a large silver dirigible. It had five leather seats, two in the front and three in the back, and an open roof. Cole helped Arthur into his seat and then everyone else piled in.

"Is everyone ready?" Gabe asked from the driver's seat. They all nodded their heads. He pressed the red ignition button on the dashboard, and, with a loud roar, the airship burst out of the shed and soared into the night air, a cold wind whipping past their faces. Gabe turned the steering wheel and they headed north, soaring over a maze of gold and silver office buildings. Most of the buildings were burning. Unable to stifle the storm brewing in his mind, Cole let go and released a torrent of hot tears. He was certain that nothing would ever be the same again.

CHAPTER FOURTEEN

Two hours later, Cole, Gabe, Brody, and Sabina were standing around Arthur's hospital bed in a cafeteria that had been converted into a makeshift convalescence area. When they had arrived at Wells Hospital, the interior was a chaotic mess – nurses in crisp white uniforms ran from patient to patient, stress pouring off them like an overbearing perfume. A third of the staff had disappeared during the bright flash, so the job of preventing the hospital from falling into chaos fell to those who remained.

Dozens of bloodied and injured people were resting in the canteen when they walked in. A nurse led them to a hospital bed, where they waited for an available doctor.

"How's the leg, Dad?" Cole asked.

Arthur winced in response and grabbed his leg. "Oh, it's not too bad."

"Hang in there, Arthur. A doctor will be here soon." Sabina leaned down and kissed his lined forehead.

"Were you able to find out anything about Jaxon?" Brody asked.

"We did," Sabina answered. She looked around, checking to see if anybody near them was listening, before continuing. "It's not much, but it's something. We did some digging into his records and learned that he was born and raised in Mechanica City. When he was about ten years old, his father killed himself. There seems to have been issues with alcohol."

"His father killed himself? But...but he said that he worked for his dad," Cole said.

"Well, I think we can all agree that Jaxon hasn't been truthful about many things. Anyway, he disappeared off the map for several years after that. He popped up again two years ago when he tried to sue the city for emotional distress."

"Emotional distress? Over what?!" Brody asked.

"That's unclear. The court files were sealed. After that, he went off the record for a second time. That's all I have. Unfortunately, none of that explains why he's attacking the city."

Cole sat down in a chair and put his head in his hands. He was desperate to solve this, but this new information only left him with more questions. Who really was Jaxon? Was that even his real name? None of it made any sense. He felt dizzy. How would they ever be able to fix this?

"What do we do now?" Gabe asked.

They all looked at each other, unsure of what to say. Several tense minutes passed.

"Well...it looks like we're going to need more information," Cole finally said, rising to his feet. "There are still too many unknowns. Where did they go? What did they change in time? The only place that can provide us with answers is Ruby's apartment."

Brody groaned. "You seriously want to go back there? That guard could kill us!"

"But we're running out of time, Brody!"

"The three of us versus one guard? That should be easy!" Gabe said.

"Well...alright. But what will you do?" Brody asked Sabina and Arthur.

"I wish that I could go with you, but it looks like I'm stuck here," Arthur said. He looked down at his damaged leg.

"I'll stay with Arthur and make sure that he's taken care of," Sabina said.

"OK. We'll come back as soon as we get more information," Cole said.

"Stay safe and stay strong, boys. You can do this," Arthur said. Cole, Brody, and Gabe waved goodbye to Arthur and Sabina before turning around and heading back to the dirigible that was parked out front. They jumped in and flew towards Ruby's apartment.

*****

Fifteen minutes later, the three boys were huddled behind a row of bushes that stood across the street from Ruby's apartment. Cole peered over the top of the bush – an armed guard was standing in front of the apartment's side entrance.

"How do we get past that guy?" Brody wondered.

"I have an idea," Cole said, and he reached in his coat pocket and took out the Invisibility

Vambrace. "I'll sneak up on the guard, take him out, and then you follow after me when the coast is clear."

"That thing can really make you invisible?" Gabe asked. Cole clasped it to his right arm, pushed the button, and his whole body disappeared in a flash. Gabe gasped.

"As soon as you see him go down, run over," Cole explained. He took a deep, steadying breath and headed straight for the guard. The guard was clothed in thick body armor and a long rifle hung from his shoulders.

Cole stepped on a twig and froze in terror. The guard whipped around.

"Who's there?" he asked, pointing his gun around him. Cole held his breath. The guard was inches away from him.

"I said, who's th --"

Before the guard could finish his sentence, Cole moved behind him and punched him in the back of the head. The guard's eyes crossed and he crumpled to the ground.

"Nice hit!" Gabe said as he and Brody ran up to Cole. They moved to the side door and disappeared inside.

They found themselves in a small entryway that opened onto a white hallway. Everything was dark and quiet. Several nondescript white doors led off the hall.

"Ugh it stinks in here," Brody groaned, covering his nose. "It's like a mix between body odor and...is that stale cigarettes? Yikes. I can't believe Ruby actually lives here."

"Do you think anyone else is here?" Gabe whispered.

"No idea," Cole whispered back. "Let's keep moving."

They walked slowly down the hallway, listening closely for any sign of movement. Cole reached for the handle on the first door – it was unlocked. They entered an empty sitting room with a square window that looked out onto the street. The floors were bare and the room was stark. Sliding wooden doors separated the room from the rest of the apartment. Along one wall was a line of large, hand drawn maps with multicolored push pins stuck to them.

"What is all of this?" Cole asked. The wide maps, covered in dark, swirling ink, stretched across the wall. Upon closer inspection, he discovered that he was looking at maps of Mechanica City. The push pins were placed over Bruckerman's, the Empress Hotel, and several other locations.

"Whatever their plan is, Project Hominum has clearly been working on it for a long time," Brody said.

They slid open the wooden door and stepped into the next room. This space was just as vacant and bleak as the previous room. Cole stared around in silent bewilderment; there were several soiled mattresses in the middle of the room, a pile of filthy clothes, and crumpled food wrappers and soda cans were scattered across the floor. One wall was covered with charcoal sketches of a very early mechanical model, while the opposite wall was plastered with photographs of Arthur and Karma. Large x's had been carved over their faces.

"What the hell..." Gabe said, grimacing as he peered at the butchered photos.

Something nagged at the back of Cole's mind as he stared at the mechanical sketches. There was something familiar about the crudely made drawings of a mechanized man.

"Why do I feel like I've seen this before? Do either of you recognize these drawings?"

Gabe shook his head. Brody walked over to the wall, stared at the photos closely for a few seconds, and then gasped.

"Actually...I do! We learned about this in my Queer Studies class. Oscar Wilde, the famous author and playwright, drew this, remember? Engineers later used his illustration as the basis for the very first mechanical design. But why the obsession with Oscar, though? I mean, I *love* his plays and he's a total queer icon, but this feels so random. Unless..."

"Unless what?" Gabe asked.

"Unless it's not random. What if Jaxon targeted him for some reason? That would explain why he hijacked *The Astrolabe*...Let me check something." Brody pulled out his phone and stared at it for several minutes.

"What are you looking for?" Cole asked anxiously.

Brody gasped and clapped his hand over his mouth. "That BASTARD. *I knew it!* Listen to this. I'm reading from Wikipedia: 'Oscar Wilde died on April 26th, 1895 at the Old Bailey while waiting for his trial to begin. Victorian doctors determined that the cause of death was loss of blood due to a stab wound, but the culprit was never discovered.' *This isn't right!* Oscar Wilde died from meningitis in 1900, not a stab wound in 1895. I guess Jaxon murdered him in order to prevent mechanicals from ever being created...and it worked."

Everyone's pockets began to vibrate. With shaking hands, they pulled out their phones -- a video message was waiting on the glass screen. Cole clicked on the link and, a second later, they were all staring at a video of a broad-shouldered man sitting behind a desk. His face was covered with a Project Hominum mask.

"Hello Mechanica City," he said. Cole's stomach burned with anger when he realized that it was Jaxon's voice. "Nice to see you again. You may have noticed that a few things have changed around here. Yes, it's true -- every disgusting robot in the world has disappeared. Many of you watching this video have reached out to Project Hominum to express your support for our cause, and for that we are deeply grateful. Look at what we've accomplished! However, there are also those who disagree with our worldview. Apparently, our methods are 'too harsh.' Well, to them I say this – get over it. You should have known that this was coming. I hope that now you're finally aware of what I'm capable of. With a snap of my fingers, I made robots disappear! Don't ever underestimate Project Hominum again."

The three boys looked at each other in alarm.

"This is just the beginning. And now that Mayor Simpson is gone, I think I'll be taking over that position. You'll get to know me very soon. Project Hominum looks forward to leading this city in a better direction."

A long and heavy silence descended upon the three crestfallen boys when the video ended. Jaxon's message was too horrific to even comprehend, let alone accept. Cole's vision blurred from his angry tears. He would never see Karma again...

"NO!" he screamed, slamming his fists into the wall. He started clawing at the pictures, furiously tearing them down and ripping them into shreds. How could he have let this happen? He had failed both Karma and Ruby...

"Cole, stop it!" Brody shouted. "We can still fix this! Calm down and listen to me -- all we have to do is travel to 1890's London and make sure that we prevent Jaxon from killing Oscar Wilde. Then, everything should go back to normal! Don't give up yet."

"You make it sound so easy, Brody, but it's not that simple! We can't do that! My dad has always told me that the past cannot be altered under *any* circumstances. If you change even *one* major event, terrible things will happen! And he was clearly right. Look at the sky! What will happen if we confront Jaxon and change something *again*?"

"What other choice do we have?" Gabe asked. "The worst has already happened! We have to set things right again. Brody's plan is the best idea that we've got."

Cole paced around the room, his mind roiling like a dark storm cloud. The weight of what they had to do was threatening to crush him.

A sharp scream came from outside. Cole moved to the window and looked down – the Project Hominum member with a piggish face was standing over the unconscious guard that Cole had taken care of earlier. Two masked guards stood next to her. The blonde guard held her gun and ran inside, the other guards following close behind.

"What do we do? That's way more guards than we expected!" Brody said, panic rising in his throat.

"We have to hide!" Gabe whispered.

Everyone's eyes flew around the room, searching desperately for a hiding place, but the room was completely bare. The voices were coming closer.

"Up there!" Cole said, pointing at the ceiling. A ceiling panel was slightly askew and black darkness peered out from its depths...

A second later, the three members of Project Hominum stormed into the room. They searched every corner of the space, long cigarettes dangling from their lips.

"I swear that I heard a noise," the blonde guard insisted. She plopped down onto one of the soiled mattresses, took a pull from her cigarette, and blew a thick cloud of acrid smoke into the air.

"There's nobody here, Parker," another guard replied brusquely. He pulled off his mask and wiped his sweaty forehead. He was tall and lanky, with a long, angular face and dark skin.

"*Obviously*," Parker replied, "but I heard what I heard."

"I still can't believe he did it. Those nasty robots are GONE!" cheered the last guard, a chubby man with a blotchy face and a wiry beard.

"Maybe there will actually be jobs open now," quipped the lanky guard. "Stupid bottom feeders...good riddance."

Right above them, tucked away inside a cramped ceiling vent, Cole, Brody, and Gabe nervously looked down upon the cackling guards below. *Bottom feeders*. The phrase caused a cold chill of disgust to roll down Cole's spine.

"So. What do we do now, Crawford?" Parker asked.

"We wait for further instructions. You ask too many questions," Crawford barked.

"Man, now that the robots are gone, we can do whatever we want. You don't look half bad, Parker. You could definitely use those skills to pay your rent," the bearded guard said, smiling lasciviously.

Parker flipped him off and tossed her cigarette at him.

A loud groan came from the ceiling.

"What was that?" Crawford asked.

"See? I told you that I heard something!" Parker said.

All three of the guards jumped to their feet and stared at the ceiling. Inside the ceiling vent, Cole, Brody, and Gabe tried to adjust their positions to redistribute their weight, but it was no use. With a loud crash, the ceiling buckled underneath them and they fell heavily to the floor in a haze of dust and broken ceiling tiles.

Cole looked up slowly at the three guards that surrounded them. "H-Hello," he said sheepishly.

CHAPTER FIFTEEN

"Who the hell are you?" Crawford roared, pointing his rifle at their faces.

"W-We, we just--" Brody stammered. The three boys slowly stood up with their hands raised in surrender. They were covered from head to toe in white dust.

"How did you get in here?" the bearded guard asked roughly.

"Why are we talking? Shoot them!" Parker screamed.

"DUCK!" Cole bellowed. The three boys hit the floor as neon green blasts of energy exploded from the guard's gun barrels. The blasts bounced around the room, pinging off the walls and smashing windows, before hitting each guard squarely in the chest. They fell heavily to the floor.

"Is everyone OK?" Brody asked. They stood up and dusted themselves off. Brody picked up the guard's fallen weapons, as well as a pair of handheld receivers, and tossed them to Cole and Gabe.

"Let's get out of here!" Gabe said. Crawford and the guard with the wiry beard were unconscious and sprawled out on the floor, but Parker was slowly stirring. She groaned in pain and scrambled to her feet.

"You...YOU ARE DEAD!"

Before she could say anything more, Brody threw his fist out and punched her in the face; she hit the floor again. "Run!" he screamed. The boys ran to a shattered window and looked down -- the sidewalk was only two stories below – they could make it.

An energy blast suddenly whistled by them and exploded above their heads -- Parker was up again. "COME BACK HERE!" she bellowed.

Without a backward glance, Cole, Brody, and Gabe climbed out of the broken window and started quickly scaling down the apartment wall.

"DIRTY RAAAAAATS!" Parker pointed her rifle through the window and furiously fired off several rounds. The boys let go of the wall and fell to the ground. Then, ducking their heads from the onslaught of energy blasts, they sprinted down the street in the direction of the manor house.

When they finally approached the house, four Project Hominum members were patrolling the front yard. Without thinking, the boys aimed their rifles and took out each of the guards before sprinting up the stairs and locking the front door behind them. Cole's heart was pounding painfully in his chest.

"OK. Let's jump on *The Astrolabe* and fix this mess," he said, struggling to catch his breath. Gabe and Brody nodded in agreement and they ran to the laboratory. Once inside, they approached the floating white door, its bright panes of stained glass glittering under the lights. Cole ran to the cupboard and took out a spare pocket watch.

"Hurry Cole!" Brody said. "We don't know if we were followed!"

Cole tossed the pocket watch into the air and a neon blue light, stretched into the shape of a key blade, formed a barrier around the watch. The device floated towards a glowing keyhole, fit itself inside, and unlocked the door, and, with a low groan, the door slowly began to open. A blinding white light poured out.

Loud and harsh voices began to trickle into the laboratory from outside.

"They're inside," Gabe whispered.

Brody moved to a large telescope that looked down onto the street below: more than a dozen Project Hominum members were standing in a line in front of the manor house. Their masked faces stared up at the line of windows.

"Ummm Cole? We've got company!" he cried.

Come on, come on... Cole thought desperately. The white door was almost open.

A barrage of gun blasts struck the windows and shattered the glass; Gabe and Brody jumped out of the way. The sounds of splintering wood and hurried steps came from downstairs -- they were trapped.

"We have to go!" Gabe urged.

The moment that the floating door had fully opened, Project Hominum kicked down the laboratory doors and rushed inside.

"RUN!" Cole screamed, and the three boys turned and ran through the entrance. They emerged inside a bright white room that stretched endlessly in every direction; it wasn't clear if either walls or a ceiling existed here. They ran towards a white train station that stood in the distance.

"We're gonna make it!" Brody screamed as they ran up the train station stairs. He moved to a clear podium that was standing at the center of the train platform and pressed a call button. A moment later, a sharp whistle rang out and a long, white train came into view. *The Astrolabe* sped along a pair of fiery, golden train tracks that had materialized in front of the station before sliding to a halt in front of the boys. One of the train doors opened and they ran inside.

"FASTER!" one of the guards screamed. They ran up the wooden platform steps and jumped into the train, their guns loaded and ready to fire.

"Holy crap!" Cole screamed as an energy blast flew over his head. It slammed into a glass chandelier hanging from the ceiling, causing it to explode in hundreds of pieces. The boys shielded their heads from the falling glass and kept running.

"What...What do we do?" Brody asked, gasping for air. His face was drenched in sweat.

"Keep pushing, we're almost to the front!" Gabe yelled, clutching the cramp in his side as they sprinted down the hallways.

"Hold on – *stop!*" Cole yelled.

They skidded to a halt. Two of the Project Hominum guards were blocking the door to the front compartment; they smiled and pulled out long knives. Right above them, Cole spotted a square ceiling hatch...

"Gabe, follow me. Brody? Take care of these two and then start the train!"

"With pleasure!" Brody fired his rifle at the guards blocking their way. Their bodies slammed against the wall and sank to the ground.

As soon as Cole and Gabe reached the roof of *The Astrolabe,* the train made a low groaning sound and began to pick up speed. A powerful breeze struck them as the train sped along the glowing tracks and into a swirling, pastel-shaded wormhole. The air around them churned and throbbed with energy.

The ceiling hatch suddenly popped open and two Project Hominum members climbed up and onto the roof. They glared at Cole and Gabe with fiery hatred in their eyes.

"How many of these guards are there?!" Gabe yelled over the wind.

Before Cole could answer, the Project Hominum members curled their hands into fists and lunged. Their assault was swift and ruthless. The taller of the two guards shrieked like an animal as they lashed out with both fists, aiming for Cole's head and face. He held up his arms to block their pummeling fists and dodged to the left, to the right, to the left again, trying to shove the guard towards the edge of the roof. They were a seasoned fighter, and Cole could feel his energy draining quickly as the minutes went on.

Next to Cole, Gabe fiercely battled the other guard. Among the chaos taking place on the roof, they were a blur of legs and fists. Gabe slammed his body into the guard and they both fell and hit the roof. Unfortunately, the guard was too fast for Gabe. They jumped to their feet and kicked him straight in the stomach. He groaned in pain and fell still.

At the sight of Gabe's unconscious body, an electric current rippled through Cole's body and he screamed with rage. He pressed the button on the Invisibility Vambrace and vanished.

"Oh, that's a fun trick. Where are you, you little bastard?!" the second guard growled. With hot rage pounding in his head, Cole ran behind them and shoved his hands into their back. The guard screamed and flew off the roof, tumbling down into the swirling expanse.

"*COWARD!*" the remaining guard screamed. They turned their masked head in every direction, ready to fight. "You can only win a fight when you've got your little armband, is that it? Well, it doesn't matter! It's all over. *Jaxon won!* Those robots ain't never coming back."

Cole's rage overwhelmed him and he turned off the Vambrace. "You stupid *pig*! What the *hell* are you talking about? Jaxon didn't win sh--"

The guard turned and shoved Cole in the chest. Caught by surprise, he lost his balance and teetered on the edge of the roof, arms flailing wildly in a desperate attempt to steady himself. At the last second, like a drowning man grasping for a life jacket, Cole grabbed the guard's arm and they went tumbling over the side.

CHAPTER SIXTEEN

The first thing that Cole registered when he regained consciousness was a pounding sensation in his head; it was sore to the touch. Groaning in pain, he slowly stood up and blearily took in his surroundings. Four wooden walls stood on every side of him, one of which was a latticed door. Unsure of what to do, he nervously pressed his hands against the door and stepped out.

When his eyes finally adjusted to the light, he gasped and his eyes grew wide. Above him soared a vaulted ceiling that was cream with olive green stripes. He was standing in the middle of a massive, stone tabernacle. Thick streams of white light beamed through tiny windows near the ceiling and rained down onto several rows of wooden seats inside the cathedral. The gray stone walls were covered with large and elegantly detailed canvases depicting the Virgin Mary and other pieces of Christian imagery. Cole took a deep breath and turned in a circle, taking it all in: the rough stone floors, the imposing pillars that soared upwards and supported the ceiling, and a wall of solid gold that glittered and shone under the light. The golden altar was dotted with small statues of kings and other pieces of extravagant Baroque ornamentation. Cole had never considered himself to be a very religious person, but in that moment, standing inside that echoing, charged space, an overwhelming sense of wonder enveloped him.

As he slowly walked through the silent cathedral, corrosive panic began to flutter in his chest. Where was he? And *when*, exactly, was he? But, without a plan, he had little else to do but walk down an echoing hallway and through a large pair of heavy wooden doors. Rays of sunlight hit him squarely in the face as he stepped outside, forcing him to shade his eyes. After living in frigid Mechanica City for so long, he wasn't prepared for so much light and heat.

A wide, stone plaza square stretched out in front of him for several yards and it was bordered on each side by stately stone buildings. A fluttering flag stood at the center of it. Mountains rose and fell in the distance.

A young woman with dark black hair and a plain dress passed by. Cole waved frantically to get her attention.

"Ma'am? This is kind of a strange question, but could you tell me where I am?"

"Qué?" she asked, confusion stretched across her face. She turned and hurried away in the opposite direction. Cole stared silently at her departing figure in ever increasing desperation – he needed to get his bearings straight.

After a moment of indecision, he walked straight down the length of the plaza, passing groups of people that dotted the square, and made his way onto a dirt street. For a while, he walked around, dazed, with little sense of direction. None of the bustling side streets that he turned onto, with their romantic iron street lamps, were recognizable to him. *Maybe I'm in Spain?* he wondered. The minutes crawled by and his level of stress increased with every step that he took down the dusty streets. Thick waves of heat poured down heavily and Cole's clothes were quickly drenched in sweat. Lines of banana trees, with large, glossy leaves, provided minimal shade to passersby.

Cole noticed that stark differences in class were openly reflected in the clothing that the people around him were wearing. Wealthy couples, the men in rigid suits and top hats and the women in floor length gowns with puffed sleeves, leisurely strolled next to working class men in wide-brimmed hats and frayed pants; towering stacks of woven baskets rested on their backs. Judging by the clothes, Cole decided that he must be in the twentieth century. But *where* and *when* in the twentieth century, he couldn't be sure.

Everyone that passed by him was speaking rapidly in Spanish. *If only Gabe was here to translate...* he thought sadly. At the thought of Gabe's name, he chastised himself for forgetting the important tool that was tucked in his jacket pocket – the handheld transceiver. He hastily pulled it out and switched it on.

"Gabe? Brody? Can you hear me? Are you there?"

Only the crackle of static answered him. His hands shook with panic. *What am I going to do now?*

He looked around and realized that he had wandered into a lively market square that was surrounded by tall, white buildings. Cole saw crowds of people inspecting wooden booths that were full of vibrant flowers and various types of vegetables. Men, women, and children stood behind the booths and proudly hawked their wares.

"*shhkk*COLE*shhkk*AREYOUTHERE?!" A crackling voice suddenly came out of the handheld transceiver. It sounded like it was coming from the bottom of a deep well.

"He-Hello? Gabe?" Cole stepped behind a stone wall so that he could surreptitiously speak into the transceiver. A man with a thick moustache walked by and looked at him curiously.

"*shhkk*WHEREARE*shhkk*TELL??"

"What?!" Cole said, a note of fear rising in his voice. "I can't understand you! Hello? Gabe?"

When there was no answer, he held the transceiver in the air, hoping that the signal might improve. A big part of him knew that this wouldn't work, but he was becoming increasingly desperate.

"Qué haces?" a deep voice barked behind him. Cole stopped inspecting the handheld transceiver and slowly turned around. A group of five men, all of them with similar expressions of deep suspicion on their hard faces, surrounded him. They were all wearing wide-brimmed sombreros and tight bolero jackets. Bullet cases stretched across their chests.

"I-I'm sorry, I don't speak Spanish..." he stammered.

"Qué haces? Es eso un arma?!" one of the armed men demanded. He pointed his Remington carbine rifle in Cole's face and Cole threw his hands up in surrender. The crowd in the market turned to stare at them.

Suddenly, a high-pitched whistle rang out. Cole whirled around and his eyes fell on a teen boy that was sitting on the back of a tan horse. He had unkempt black hair, large eyes, and a smug grin plastered across his face. Inexplicably, the young man had corralled all the armored men's horses next to him. Cole's stomach dropped when he noticed a shiny object hanging around the boy's neck – the pocket watch!

How did he get that? he wondered.

"Tus caballos estan sueltos!" the stranger bellowed. He slapped the backside of the horse that was closest to him and it took off down the street; the rest of the horses followed suit, racing after the spooked creature. The armed men screamed in anger and ran after their horses.

"Hey! You stole my pocket watch!" Cole yelled.

"Farewell, friend! Thank you for the gift!" the boy shouted. With a parting wave, he pulled on the reins and fled the market square.

English? Cole thought, the stranger's words hitting his ears like a comforting song playing on the radio. But any good feelings that he had quickly dissolved upon his realization that he was now out of a pocket watch. How was he going to get it back? And would he be able to find the young boy? With no other options, he swallowed the rage that was ballooning in his stomach and begrudgingly made his way down the street in the direction of the watch thief.

For the next hour, Cole wandered the streets aimlessly and searched for the thief, rivers of sweat pouring off his forehead and into his eyes. There was no sign of the smug-looking boy anywhere. *What am I going to tell Dad?* He wondered. *That little bastard could be anywhere by now!* With each labored step, Cole felt weaker and weaker. His thoughts were becoming increasingly scattered and slow because of the heat.

He wandered down a side street and then turned a corner onto a wide alleyway. Two elderly women were sweeping their stoops with wooden brooms. An iron bench was positioned against the wall, so Cole plopped himself down onto it to rest his aching feet. He shrugged off his jacket and wearily wiped the sweat off his face. At this point, his situation was becoming dire. If he didn't find shelter or water soon, he was going to pass out.

A familiar voice, loud and sarcastic, suddenly came from the end of the alleyway. Another market square, full of wooden booths, was located a few feet away. With hot anger pounding in his head, Cole gathered his remaining strength and entered the square.

The thief was easy to locate – he was having a loud argument with a bearded man standing behind a vendor booth. The pocket watch was dangling from his hand.

"Mentiroso! Esto es real! Maldito sea!" he yelled in exasperation. The bearded man stepped out from behind the booth and furiously shooed him away, so the thief turned and started walking in the opposite direction. Cole's hands balled into fists and he ran after him.

"HEY! Give me back my watch!" He grabbed the thief by the shirt collar and shoved him into a nearby stone wall. Despite his shock and alarm, the thief kept his smug expression fixed to his face.

"Qué?" he asked innocently.

"I know you speak English!" Cole yelled back. "Give me my watch!"

"I don't know what you're speaking of!" the thief said. Cole growled and shoved him into the wall again.

"Ay, dios mío! Is this how you treat the one who saved your life? For shame!"

"You didn't save me. I...I had everything under control!"

"Of course you did," the thief quipped. "Here, take the estúpido watch. It's useless, anyway. Everyone that I tried to sell it to said that it's fake."

As he moved to hand over the pocket watch, there was a shout from across the market square. The armed men in sombreros had returned for the thief. "Estás arrestado!" they shouted, rifles raised high in the air.

The thief yelped in shock, turned, and ran down the square. Cole watched him scramble underneath a parked carriage and disappear.

The armed men slowed to a halt in front of Cole. "Adónde fue?" they barked. He didn't know what they were saying, but the meaning was perfectly clear.

"He, um, he went that way!" he said, pointing down a random alleyway. The armed men ran in that direction and disappeared.

As soon as the coast was clear, the thief scrambled out from underneath the carriage and ran over to Cole.

"Gracias, mi hermano! You just saved me from a terrible beating. Here. Take your pocket watch." He put the time piece in Cole's hand.

"Well, listen. I need you to answer something for me," Cole said. "Where am I?"

The thief stared at him quizzically. "You don't know? This is Mexico City."

Cole felt like his stomach had abruptly liquified. He swayed where he stood.

"Me-Mexico City? Well, what year is it?"

"1907. April 11th, to be exact. Are you alright, my friend? You look quite pale..."

Cole struggled to contain the rush of terror coursing through him. *How will Gabe and Brody find me now?* Black spots bloomed in front of his eyes.

"I...I feel a bit sick..." And with that, Cole's eyes rolled in the back of his head and he collapsed to the ground. The thief's mouth fell open in shock as he stared at Cole's unconscious form. He shook his head.

"OK amigo. I guess you're coming with me." The thief bent down and picked up Cole. He tossed him over his shoulder and carried him over to his horse. After securing him into the saddle, the thief jumped on and they galloped down the street.

CHAPTER SEVENTEEN

The sound of horse hooves clopping on the ground filled Cole's ears as he regained consciousness. His eyes fluttered open and he found himself swaying side to side on the back of a horse.

"Ah! You're finally awake. Here, drink this." The thief turned around and handed Cole a leather satchel. He snatched it up with greedy hands and took several long gulps of the clear water inside. It was as if he was ingesting liquid sunlight; the moment that the water touched his lips, he instantly felt more clear-headed and his muscles began to unclench.

"What...What happened?" he asked after several minutes of silence. The water satchel was nearly empty.

"You fainted. Hit the ground quite hard."

"I did? How long have I been out?"

"We've been riding for about an hour. We're almost to my home. You can rest there."

As Cole slowly regained his strength, he marveled at the sights that surrounded them. Donkeys carrying boxes on their backs, as well as glossy, horse-drawn carriages, passed by on the street. Stray dogs with wide smiles on their faces patrolled the sidewalks for scraps. Rows of sand-colored, stone buildings with regal columns seemed to rise out of the ground on either side of the street, staggering over each other as if they were struggling to lay claim to the same stretch of land. Cole had never seen anything like it before.

The thief pulled out a hand-rolled cigarette and lit it with a match. "So...what's your name?"

"Cole. What's yours?"

"My name is Hector and this is Narciso." He chuckled lightly and gently patted his horse on the neck. "He acts like he's shy, but he's actually quite full of himself, hence the name. Welcome to Ciudad de México! Where are you from?"

Cole struggled to think of an answer that didn't sound completely insane. "Oh, you know...here and there."

"Alright, forget I asked," Hector laughed.

"Are you from America?" Cole asked.

"No, but my Ma was. She taught me English. My Pa was from here." He tugged on the reins and steered Narciso towards a wooden hitching post that stood in front of a stately, two-story estate that had a copper roof that was an ochre color. The entire building was a block long, and thin trees with large palms flanked the entrance. Cole could see several people moving around an open courtyard.

"Here we are!" Hector said. They jumped off Narciso's back and Hector tied him to the hitching post.

"Do all of these people work here?" Cole asked as they walked by men and women sweeping the courtyard or making repairs to the tiled floor.

"We all live and work here," Hector explained. "All haciendas are like that."

"What's a hacienda?"

"A hacienda is like a plantation. Actually, it's more like a factory. We're hired to grow wheat, fruits, vegetables. We also make leather and tallow. Whatever is required. In return, we are allowed to live here. It's not the easiest life, but it keeps my sister and I off the streets. The patrón is a kind man."

Hector talked nonstop as he led Cole through the hacienda. Cole's spirits rose due to the homespun warmth that seemed to emanate from the walls. Many attractive and rustic details caught his eye: doors carved out of Spanish cedar, arched hallways, exposed ceiling beams, and bright textiles that hung from the white stucco walls. Then, they took a tour of the courtyard, with its charming stone fountain, before ending with a quick look at the backyard. Cole observed a line of farmers tilling the land.

Fifteen minutes later, Cole followed Hector into a large kitchen where a group of women were slicing cutlets of chicken for dinner. A teen girl with twin black braids and a cowboy hat was sitting at a table. She drank deeply from a flask.

"Elena, there you are! My beautiful sister!" Hector said. Elena put down her flask and scrutinized Cole with a stern expression on her face. Her gaze was steely and unreadable. She had brown skin that was the color of cinnamon.

"Who is this?"

"This is Cole! He helped me escape from the rurales at the market and he needs a place to stay."

"Space is limited here," she grumbled. "You know that. There's hardly enough room for us as it is."

"Don't worry, I won't stay long. Just for the night," Cole assured her. He had no idea if this was a true statement, but he couldn't afford to think too far ahead. His plan was forming minute by minute.

"Why did the rurales come after you?" Elena asked.

"Well..." Hector replied sheepishly. "Don't worry about it. It's a long story."

"Hector! What have I told you about making them angry? You are going to get yourself killed!"

"Oh, hermana. You worry too much! I was just having a bit of fun. So, what do you say about Cole?"

Elena pounded the table with her fist. "Moldito sea! What about the...the *situation* that we're currently dealing with? Huh?"

They fell silent for several seconds, a tense look passing between the two siblings. The women that were cooking dinner paused to see what would happen next.

"Elena! We've been dealing with that for years. Nothing bad will happen," Hector pleaded.

After a moment, Elena shrugged her shoulders in resignation and took another swig from her flask.

"Fine. He can stay. You look awful, Cole. Have some caldo de pollo."

One of the women preparing food kindly handed Cole a ceramic bowl that was filled with savory chicken, sliced carrots, a corn cob, and thick broth. The delicious smell made Cole dizzy – he suddenly realized how ravenous he was. He sat down at the table and started to shovel the soup into his mouth.

"I guess I should thank you for helping my idiota brother," Elena said. "You can rest in his room."

Cole nodded, his mouth full of food. When he finally swallowed the last bite of the warm caldo de pollo, he sat back with his hands on his stomach, finally starting to feel normal again. As if he'd ingested a sleeping tonic, exhaustion descended on him and it was suddenly a struggle to keep his eyes open. After thanking everyone for the food, he stood up and Hector led him down a hallway and into a small, plain bedroom.

"I really appreciate this. Oh, by the way, how old is your sister? Should she be drinking?" Cole asked.

Hector shook his head and laughed. "You're a strange man, Cole. I'll wake you up in a few hours." He smiled and left the room. Cole laid down on the bed and, before his head even hit the pillow, he was asleep.

CHAPTER EIGHTEEN

It felt like only seconds had passed before Cole was being roughly shaken awake. He slowly opened his eyes and saw Hector standing over him with an excited grin on his face and a large sombrero in his hands.

"Well rested, mi amigo? I hope so, because we are going to the bull fight!"

Cole rubbed his eyes and stared at him groggily. "The...the what?"

"The bull fight! Come on!" He dragged Cole out of bed. They hurried downstairs and passed by Elena in the courtyard. She was cleaning her rifle and smoking a cigarette.

"Miguel is looking for you. I think he needs help with mucking out the stables," she called after Hector.

"I'll do it later! We can't miss the bullfight!"

"Ay, dios mío! *Another* one?"

"Oh, callarse!" Hector laughed. "Cole has never seen one before, right?"

Cole shook his head.

"Well, don't blame me if Miguel is mad at you later," she said. "Don't be late for dinner!"

The two boys turned and left the kitchen.

"So, um, how far away is this bull fight?" Cole asked while Hector untied Narciso from the hitching post. He wasn't exactly thrilled to be leaving the hacienda. Frankly, he'd much rather spend his time trying to fix his handheld transceiver. But what other choice did he have? "Very close. In the Toreo de la Condesa," Hector replied. "It was built this year. I love it! Oh, you'll need this." He handed Cole the sombrero and he put it on his head – the sun disappeared and he instantly felt cooler. They jumped onto Narciso's back and galloped off in the direction of the bullring.

After a hair-raising ride through the city, they finally stopped on a patch of grass in front of the Toreo de la Condesa. It was a plain and spartan, yet imposing, stone amphitheater with metal staircases running up the exterior. These staircases were packed with lines of people trying to get inside the bullring. Colorful posters with swirling Spanish text were splashed across a squat, white wall that ran in front of the arena. Cole's eyes grew wide as he heard the roar of thousands of cheering spectators.

"Wow! You know, we actually have something like this back home. It's for dirigible racing, though. This is fantastic!" Cole gushed.

"What's a dirigible?" Hector asked.

"Oh. Um...don't worry about it."

They followed the dense and conservatively dressed crowd up the stairs and into the stadium. It was a wide, circular amphitheater with an open top that allowed the blazing sun to come pouring in. Cole stared around in awe at the thousands of people that were packed into the rows of hard stone seats. At the center of the bullring, he could see a circular space that served as the stage for the bull fight. The area was covered with a layer of crushed, tan rocks. A tall, wooden barrier with locked doors circled the edge of the bullring, and Cole assumed that this was the waiting area for the bullfighters.

"Let's get to our seats," Hector said. "I apologize that we will be sitting in the sun, but they were the cheapest option. The sombrero will help." They began to climb the stone staircase towards a section of seating near the middle of the stadium. Despite the bizarre circumstances that Cole now found himself in, he felt a small sliver of curiosity and excitement for the impending bull fight.

"What's that on the walls?" he asked when they sat down in their seats. He pointed to a series of footholds in the walls.

"Those are used by el personal during an emergency," Hector explained.

Cole's face blanched. *An emergency?*

"Look, it's the presidente!" Hector pointed to a booth that sat near the top of the stadium. A man with a top hat and a curled, black moustache rose to his feet and waved to the boisterous crowd down below – the bull fight had begun.

A tall and handsome matador, along with a group of men clad in colorful attire, strode confidently into the center of the bullring to the roar of the crowd. A jaunty military march began to play. The matador was wearing a tight-fitting uniform called the traje de luces, or 'suit of lights.' It was blood red with spectacular gold embroidery that sparkled under the sun's gaze. The group of men walked to the edge of the bullring and held out their hands to the audience; a strong and dramatic pose. The crowd responded with even more feverish excitement.

"Who are those men with the matador?" Cole asked.

"They are his assistants. The men on the horses are the picadores and the three other men are called the banderilleros."

A gate was suddenly thrown open and a hulking bull came charging into the bullring. His large, muscular body was covered in sleek, black fur and wickedly sharp horns protruded from the sides of his bulky head. The bull snorted and stamped his feet angrily.

The matador turned and faced the bull head on. He pulled off his magenta cape and, with a flourish, he whipped it around and held it out for the bull. The bull snorted, leaned down, and then charged the fluttering cape. At the last second, the matador skillfully stepped out of the way and the beast galloped past him, kicking up a cloud of dirt. With a wide smile, the matador struck a pose and waved to his adoring fans.

The bull abruptly changed direction and barreled back towards the matador. Without missing a beat, he whipped the flowing cape around and made the bull pass through it again. They continued this dance for the next several minutes; a series of taunts, the bull charged, the matador deflected him.

A sharp bugle blast rang out, signaling the start of the next phase of the bull fight. The matador left the center of the bullring, allowing his assistants to take his place. One of the picadors readjusted the sharp lance in his hand and aimed it squarely at the bull's shoulders. His horse was draped in a long, protective covering that shielded it from the bull's horns.

For the next several minutes, the picador slowly circled the bull, his eyes narrowed in concentration, and the bull stared back in silent rage. With a swift movement, the picador leaned forward and thrust out the lance, sinking the metal deep into the bull's muscular shoulder. The animal shrieked in pain and a river of blood poured out of the wound. He stomped his hooves and reared back, droplets of blood scattering across the dirt floor. Cole's stomach churned at the sight of the wounded animal. In his world, animals could almost always be repaired, but this organic bull was surely about to die soon.

Hector watched the color drain from Cole's face and he chuckled. "Come now, mi amigo! You've got to have a stronger stomach for this!" Cole wanted to argue back, but he stayed silent in order to be polite.

"Now it is time for the tercio de banderillas," Hector explained as a second bugle blast rang out. The banderilleros ran towards the bull, barbed swords drawn, and tried to stab as much of the bull's exposed neck as possible. The crowd was going crazy at this point. To Cole, it looked like the men and the bull were locked in an intimate dance with each other, a violent and bloodthirsty pas de deux. There was a strange and unexpected beauty to their fluid movements. The banderilleros twirled and spun on their heels, narrowly avoiding the bull's pointed horns.

The matador eventually left the sidelines and jumped back into the fray, swinging his capote around with a flourish. The bull savagely knocked one of the banderilleros to the ground and whirled around to face the matador, taking deep, ragged breaths. Cole was amazed that the creature was still standing.

Like a thin wisp of smoke, a quiet voice reached Cole's ears. "Cole? Hello?"

"What did you say?" he asked.

"I didn't say anything," Hector replied.

"Cole? Are you there?" the voice said again. There was a buzz in his pants pocket, and when he reached inside he pulled out the source of the voice – the handheld transceiver! He instantly forgot about everything that was going on around him and jumped to his feet.

"Um, I-I'll be right back!"

"But you're going to miss--" Hector protested, but Cole never heard what it was that he was going to miss because he sprinted down the stone steps, maneuvered past a crowd of excited spectators, and spotted a secluded corner to stand in.

"Can you hear me? Hello?" he asked. The radio signal crackled and popped. There was a brief silence. Then, like soft music emerging from the bottom of a well, Gabe's voice surfaced.

"*Cole*! You're alive! I didn't think that I would ever hear your voice again!" he cried, his low voice cracking with emotion. Hot tears poured out of Cole's eyes as his legs buckled underneath him and he sank against the stone wall, overwhelmed with relief.

"God, I miss you. Are you and Brody OK?"

"Yeah, we're completely fine. But how are *you*? Are you safe?"

"It's a really long story, but I'm OK. Right now, I'm with this guy named Hector who is helping me out."

"Where are you? And who is this Hector guy?" Gabe asked quizzically.

"Don't worry, he's fine," Cole said. "I'm stuck in Mexico City. April 11th, 1907, to be exact.

"Well, that's lucky. We just passed the 1920's. But how will we find you?"

"I'm staying at a hacienda thirty minutes outside the city. It's the first one that you'll see, you can't miss it! How is *The Astrolabe?* Did Project Hominum damage it?"

"*The Astrolabe* is fine. Project Hominum can't stop us," Gabe said. "Hold on and we'll be there as soon as we can. I love you!"

Cole wiped the tears from his eyes and beamed with elation. "I love you too. See you soon!"

"You almost missed the end!" Hector said as soon as Cole had returned to his seat. The matador was standing in the center of the bullring, his back elongated and rigid, and he was now brandishing a red capote in one hand and a steel sword in the other. The tension inside the stadium had reached a fever pitch. The matador waved the capote and danced out of the way of the bull once again. He lifted his sword high in the air, preparing to strike the killing blow. Cole covered his eyes.

The matador ran and lunged at the bull, aiming his sword at a vulnerable patch of flesh near the bull's neck; the beast galloped straight for him. At the last second, the bull slid to a halt and thrust its horns up and forward. The matador tried to leap out of the way, but the bull caught him in the backside. He was tossed into the air, flipping head over feet like a limp rag doll, before crashing spectacularly onto the ground. For a moment, it looked like he was going to be able to scramble to his feet and start the fight again. However, as soon as he lifted his head, his eyes crossed and he fainted. The audience groaned.

"Is it over?" Cole asked.

"Let us see what the crowd decides," Hector replied. "If they believe that the matador performed admirably and skillfully, they will kill the bull and give one of his ears to the matador!"

Cole grimaced in response.

"However, the bull put up quite a good fight, so they might pardon him. Keep watching!"

For several tense minutes, the presidente conferred with the group of people standing around him. "*Indulto! Indulto!*" the crowd screamed. They threw out their hands, a tidal wave of white handkerchiefs rolling among the stands. The floor vibrated under Cole's feet.

The presidente finally turned to face the crowd and thrust both of his hands into the air – the bull would be spared! An explosion of joyful screams erupted in the bullring; it sounded like a bomb had been detonated. The ecstatic crowd jumped up and down and stomped their feet in celebration. Fistfuls of bright flowers were tossed into the air as the bull was paraded around the bullring before being led out of the stadium. Cole, enjoying the warm sun falling on his face, laughed joyfully and caught one of the flowers that fell like snow around him. Everything would be fine now. He was going to be saved!

*****

The sun was sinking behind the mountains by the time that they returned to the hacienda. While Hector led Narciso to the stables for the night, Cole listened to the loud laughter and music that trickled out of the hacienda. All the lights were on and a raucous celebration was going on inside.

"What is everyone celebrating?" he asked Hector when he returned.

"Well, it has been quite a long week, so tonight we celebrate our hard work!" Hector explained cheerfully. "You will love it. Follow me!"

As soon as they walked into the kitchen, a large group of hacienda employees turned around and greeted them jovially. Everyone was smiling and full of energy; their lively chatter filled the room. Long, wooden tables had been pushed together and they sagged under the weight of colorful dishes such as chilaquiles, pozole, crispy tostadas, as well as savory elote covered in Cotija cheese. Cole's stomach grumbled in response – everything looked amazing. A woman wearing an apron and a warm smile waved Cole over and she handed him a plate that was piled high with flautas and guacamole. The atmosphere was warm and inviting and, for the first time since he had arrived in Mexico City, Cole was finally able to relax and enjoy himself.

The hours slipped away, and by the time that most of the staff had eaten their fill and retired to their rooms for the night, Cole, Elena, and Hector were still going strong. They moved to the courtyard and sat underneath the velvety night sky, drinking tequila and sharing stories. The two siblings pelted Cole with several personal questions, each one more intrusive than the last, but Cole played coy and improvised a flimsy story about being a traveling salesman making his way through Mexico.

"Wait a minute, your father chased you with what?!" Cole asked, laughing and trying his best not to choke on his drink. Elena had just told a hilarious story about what happened when Hector had accidentally knocked over a chicken carcass that his father was dressing.

"*With the chicken carcass!*" Hector replied. "He swung it at my head and chased me all over the kitchen. Feathers were everywhere!" Their laughter blended with a soothing melody that floated out of a nearby window. One of the staff members, a man with hairy arms and a thick neck, strummed a romantic guitar melody for a group of enamored female staff members.

"At least *your* father brought food home!" Elena quipped.

"Are you step-siblings?" Cole asked.

"Half-siblings. We share the same mother," Elena explained. "Mi padre was a gringo bastardo from Wyoming. He left her when she got pregnant with me – no honor at all. Anyway, she brought me back to the city where she met another puta, his father. He ran out on her, too." She pulled out a hand-rolled cigarette and put it to her lips. There was a strained silence.

"Wow. I'm really sorry," Cole said.

"Ma didn't meet very many nice men," Hector replied.

"Where is your mother now?"

Hector and Elena exchanged a tense glance.

"She died a few years ago," Elena explained.

"She was *murdered,* you mean," Hector mumbled. Cole's eyes flew open in shock.

"Someone murdered her?!"

"Hector exaggerates, but a broken heart and a life of back-breaking work did send her to an early grave."

"To Ma!" Hector exclaimed, holding his tequila glass out.

"May she rest in peace!" Elena replied. All three of them clinked their glasses together and drank their tequila; the liquid burned Cole's throat.

"My mom passed away, too, but I can't imagine also losing my dad." Arthur's face appeared in his mind's eye, and he felt a rush of gratitude for never giving up on finding him.

"Anyway, then we got a job with this hacienda, and --" Hector said.

A blast of gunfire erupted out of the darkness; the music inside the hacienda abruptly stopped. They all turned to look in the direction of the gunshots.

"What was that?" Cole asked. Despite the darkness and the low lights, he could see that Elena and Hector's faces were twisted with foreboding. Something in the air had shifted.

"He finally found us again," Elena whispered.

"What? Who is looking for you?" Cole asked, but Hector and Elena simply stood up and raced out of the courtyard. Cole followed closely behind.

CHAPTER NINETEEN

"Where are we going?" Cole asked as he followed Hector and Elena up to the second floor of the hacienda. Three women in black maid uniforms ran screaming past them.

"What is happening?!*"*

"Stay quiet and follow me!" Elena barked, and they ran down a hallway, turned the corner, and stumbled into a small storage room. Stacks of wooden crates filled the cramped space. Elena and Hector crouched down and crawled over to the window.

"You better tell me what's going --"

"Move away from the window!" Hector demanded. Cole crouched down and moved next to him.

"Do you see that man with the bowler hat down there?" Elena asked. She peered out of the window, pointing to the front yard down below. Through the darkness, Cole could just make out a group of five men standing in front of the hacienda. They were all wearing similar outfits: dark, shabby suit jackets and pants, waistcoats with pocket watches hanging off the fabric, and black bowler hats that were cocked to the side.

"ELENAAA!" shouted out a man who was standing in front of the gang. He looked like he was in his early forties, with small eyes, a square jaw, and pale eyebrows. A sneer ran across his mouth.

"Who is that man?" Cole asked nervously. The man's twisted smile sent a chill down his spine.

"You don't recognize him from the wanted posters?" Elena asked.

"No, I...I must have missed those."

"That's Butch Cassidy and his Hole-in-the-Wall Gang," she answered grimly.

"BUTCH CASSIDY?!" Cole shouted. "Um, you could say that I've heard a few things about him. What does he want?"

"ELENA! Now, where is my sweet daughter? COME OUT HERE RIGHT NOW!"

Did he just say 'daughter?' Cole's stomach filled with icy dread. He looked at her and her face drained of color.

"How did he find me?" she whispered.

"Butch Cassidy is your father?" Cole exclaimed, but he didn't hear Elena's response because at that moment, the patrón of the hacienda walked out of the front doors and approached the smirking criminal. He was a portly man with a large stomach and a bald head. For several tense minutes, the two men spoke, but Cole, Hector, and Elena were too far away to hear what they were saying.

"The patrón will make them leave," Hector said. "He is a very strong man."

Shouts came from below. Butch Cassidy had gotten right up into the patrón's face, and the two men started to raise their voices aggressively. A shoving match ensued, and then Butch threw his fist out and connected with the side of the patrón's face; the plump man was roughly thrown backwards and landed on the ground. He remained motionless.

"*MIERDA!*" Hector yelled. He and Cole started to panic.

"*What are we going to do now?*"

"We need to escape!"

"Are they going to kill us?"

"ENOUGH!" Elena barked, and Hector and Cole fell silent. "Do exactly what I tell you to do, OK? We're going to go downstairs and pick up something from my bedroom. Then we'll find a place to hide in the city until things are safe. Is that clear?"

"Is that where --?" Hector started to say.

"Let's go!" She jumped to her feet and ran out of the room, Hector trailing behind. Cole still didn't know what was going on, but, without a better plan, he had no choice but to run after them.

Carefully and quietly, with their breath held, Elena, Hector, and Cole moved down the short staircase in the entrance hall and hovered on the bottom step. Elena pulled out a small revolver from the inside of her boot and held it out in front of her.

There was a loud *bang* and screams to the right of the stairs. When they peeked over the railing, they could see that Butch and his gang had broken into the hacienda and were wandering around the dining room. They filled the space with their cruel, barking laughter as they kicked over ceramic pots and tied up staff members that they found hiding in the room.

"I'M GONNA FIND YOU, ELENA!" Butch shouted, and the gang of men continued knocking over furniture and wreaking havoc.

I have to warn Brody and Gabe. I can't let them walk into this! Cole thought.

Suddenly, two men who worked for the hacienda kicked open a door and burst into the dining room, rifles drawn. Cole, Hector, and Elena ducked behind the staircase as several gun shots went off, popping like fireworks. For several seconds, there was nothing but the sound of bullets raining down. Then, silence fell. They looked over the railing again and their hearts sank: two bodies were laying on the floor and Butch and his gang were nowhere to be found.

"Now is our chance. Follow me!" Elena whispered. Crouched down, everyone crossed the empty dining room, ran down a hallway, and stopped in front of a wooden door. Elena unlocked it and they hurried inside.

"You still have it, right?" Hector asked. They were standing in a small, plain bedroom that contained a bed, a wooden trunk, and a small table with a water basin and a lantern sitting on top of it.

"Of course!" Elena responded. She kneeled in front of the bed, lifted the mattress, and started digging around.

"I still don't understand why Butch Cassidy is looking for you," Cole said. "Attacking this hacienda seems like a strange way of organizing a family reunion."

"Because of this," Elena answered. From under the mattress, she pulled out a slinky, metal chain and held it up to the lantern light. A large sapphire dangled from the silver necklace; it looked very heavy. Cole reeled back in shock.

"Wow, that's beautiful. Where did you get it?"

"It belonged to our Ma," Elena explained. "Before she died, she gave this to me and told me to keep it safe. As you can see, it's worth a lot of money."

"I never thought this day would happen," Hector groaned.

"Pa is here to take the necklace back," Elena said. "When he robbed a bank many years ago, he stole it and gave this to my Ma as a gift. Then, when she came back to Mexico, she took the necklace with her as punishment for his refusal to marry her. He was furious. She always meant to sell it, but she never needed to. We have to make sure he doesn't get it."

"But *why*? Why can't you just give it to him? If you haven't sold it by now, you clearly don't need it. He'll take the necklace and leave!" Cole asked.

"This is the only thing that I have left of my mother! Don't be ridiculous."

"And don't be naïve," Hector said. "He'll never leave us alive. That is not what Butch Cassidy does. He doesn't forgive easily."

The floorboards outside creaked and groaned – someone was there. Everyone froze and stared at the door.

"What do we do?" Cole mouthed. Hector held a finger to his lips and slowly tip toed to the door. He gingerly pressed his ear to it and listened; there was ragged breathing on the other side. The door handle rattled. Cole's body felt numb with panic -- would the door hold?

The doorknob finally stopped rattling and they could hear footsteps walking away. Hector released a sigh of relief. "We're safe."

With a thunderous cracking sound, the door was kicked open and two gang members from the Hole-in-the-Wall Gang entered the bedroom. With no thought for his own safety, Hector leaped at the man that was closest to him and started pummeling his face and head with his fists. The gang member was obviously much stronger than the young boy, and so Hector was quickly dispatched with a punch to the stomach.

"HECTOR!" Elena screamed, jumping to her feet. She held up her revolver, aimed, and fired; the bullet hit one of the men in the shoulder. He clutched the entry wound and fell to the floor, shrieking in pain. She tried to take out the second man, but he was too fast. He caught her by her wrist and tried to snatch the gun out of her hand. They struggled for several minutes, snarling and kicking, slamming each other into the walls. Cole jumped onto the man's back and tried to slap and punch him, but, in all the chaos, he couldn't get in a hit. The man tossed Cole over his shoulder and he slammed against the floor. His vision blurred and everything went black.

*****

Cole slowly came to. His head was throbbing and a line of dried blood ran out of his nose. He tried to use his hands, but quickly realized that they were tied behind his back with thick rope. Looking around, he could see that he was sitting on a circular patch of dirt next to a line of dense trees; Elena and Hector were on the ground next to him. Cole turned his head and he could see the hacienda off in the distance.

Hector slowly stirred next to him.

"Qué...Qué pasó? Where are we?"

"Stay quiet," Cole whispered. His heart pounded in his chest as he looked around -- Butch and the Hole-in-the-Wall Gang had to be close by. There was movement at the corner of his eye; he turned his head and saw several shadowy bodies emerging from the dark forest. As they came closer, Cole could see that it was Butch and his gang.

"Are y'all awake?" Butch asked. He kicked Elena and she came to with a start. "Good to see ya, kid. It's been a long time."

"It could have been longer," Elena spat. Butch chuckled and squatted down right in front of her, staring into her eyes.

"Now, you're gonna tell me where it is, or I'll kill ya and find it myself. It's that simple. Understand?" Butch said gruffly.

"I told you this the last time that you asked me – *I don't have it*. Ma must have sold it before she died. Accept it!" Elena yelled, but she wouldn't meet Butch's gaze.

"Hey! Sundance! Come over here," Butch said, snapping his fingers. A gang member with greased hair, a stern face, and a pointed brown moustache stepped forward.

This is the 'infamous' Sundance Kid? Cole was expecting a swaggering cowboy, or someone that looked much fiercer. This man, as well as the rest of Butch's gang, looked like he worked in a Victorian office building.

"Maybe this will change your mind," the Sundance Kid said. He walked over to Hector and hit him in the face. The young boy wailed in pain and fell back onto the ground.

"STOP IT! *I DON'T HAVE IT!*" Elena screamed.

"*Wh-Why are you doing this?!*" Cole asked, his voice cracking with fear. Butch looked over at him, stood up, and straightened his bowler hat.

"Well, times are changin'. It's gotten tough around here. I need money and I aint gonna lie about it. So, I'm gonna get that necklace and get the hell out of here. And I'm not leaving until I get it."

"We-We don't have --"

"Stop. LYING!" Butch roared. "You take me for a fool? I'm not askin' again. Tell me right now or I'm shootin' all of y'all." He pulled out a revolver and put the gun barrel to Elena's temple.

"You're really going to shoot your own daughter?" Cole asked. He had learned in school that Butch Cassidy was a criminal, but this situation was quickly spiraling out of control. The man was a psychopath.

"You don't think that I would? Kid, you don't know me very well. Which surprises me, since my picture is posted all over this country. And yeah, so maybe I am this here little girl's father, but I aint never raised her. That's gotta count for somethin'." He turned and looked at Elena again, pressing the revolver harder against her temple. "I told your mother that everything was fine as long as she didn't get pregnant. And what'd she do? She got pregnant."

Tears poured down Elena's face. "F-Fine...just take it. It doesn't matter anymore. The necklace is in my boot."

"See? That wasn't so hard." Butch yanked off her shoe and the silver necklace spilled out and landed on the ground. He grabbed it and held it up, his face shining with triumph.

"*Damn*, this sure is a beaut. I've been waitin' to hold this for such a long ti – AHHHHHH!" Butch screamed in shock and anger as a loud gunshot rang out. He jerked his hand back and dropped the necklace, and Cole could see that the piece of jewelry was now cracked and mutilated from the gunshot. Butch clutched his bloody hand and grimaced.

A barrage of bullets began to hit the ground that surrounded them. Cole screamed and laid on the ground, squeezing his eyes shut in an attempt to block out the chaos that had suddenly erupted around him. His ears rang from the deafening gun blasts. Butch Cassidy and the Hole-in-the-Wall Gang screamed in rage and shot into the darkness, towards the hacienda. They fired their guns at random, unable to see who was shooting at them.

"AHHHH AHHH AHHH!" Cole screamed. A bullet just missed his hand and hit the dirt next to him.

"Boys, I can't see nuthin'!" Butch yelled. He ducked as a bullet flew over his shoulder. "We-We gotta get out of here! Meet in the woods!" He turned and ran towards the line of trees, the rest of his gang following behind him. They were soon swallowed up by the darkness.

"Someone's coming!" Hector shouted.

Now that the bullets had finally stopped flying, Cole could hear the soft clop of horse hooves. An orange light floated towards them. Cole's heart was pounding painfully in his chest. *Who is coming?*

"Estás bein?" said a voice. Out of the darkness appeared the man that Cole had seen serenading a group of women with this guitar. He held a lantern in his left hand while he steered his horse over to the patch of dirt and jumped off.

"We...We're fine," Elena said, confusion written on her face. She was trembling. "But, Jose, what are you doing here?"

"My name isn't Jose. It's Miguel. I'm here to save you." He pulled out a switch blade and sliced the thick rope that bound Elena's hands behind her back. He did the same for Hector and Cole.

"My apologies for the subterfuge, but it was necessary. I work for the Pinkerton Agency. We're a private security and detective agency. We've been tracking Butch Cassidy and his gang for many years."

Elena walked over to the necklace and picked it up off the ground. "It's...It's worthless now. He won't be coming back anymore," she said, and tears filled her eyes and ran slowly down her cheeks. She brought her hands up to her face and began to sob silently, for herself, for her dead mother, for the father that would never care for her in the way that she wanted – all of it. And with that, Hector walked her back to the hacienda, Cole and Miguel following closely behind.

Two hours later, Cole, Hector, and Elena recovered from their traumatic night inside the kitchen. The entire hacienda staff was crammed inside the room and everyone looked pale and shell shocked. Heaping plates of tamales had been passed around, and this had done wonders for morale; everyone felt grateful to be alive. Miguel stood among the crowd, and he was joined by more members of the Pinkerton Agency. When Cole, Hector, and Elena were being led back to the hacienda, four men wearing cowboy hats suddenly materialized out of the shadows; they had been hiding out in secret locations close to the hacienda.

"Someone's coming!" a Pinkerton agent said as he looked out of the window. Everything stopped and the room filled with tension.

Did Butch come back? Cole thought to himself.

"We'll take care of this," Miguel said sternly. "Come on, boys!" The group of agents flung open the front door, rifles raised, and rushed outside.

"Lower your weapons!" a low voice said. "We're here for Cole!"

Cole jumped up from the kitchen table and ran to the window – he knew that voice!

"I'M HERE!" He shoved past the Pinkerton agents standing in the front door and ran outside. His heart soared as his eyes fell on the figure of his boyfriend. They ran to each other and embraced, wrapping their arms tightly around each other. Brody was sitting on a grey horse a foot away.

"You saved me!" Cole cried. Heavy tears made streaks in the dust that coated his cheeks. Brody jumped off his horse and all three of them cried and hugged one another. There were rivers of tears and much jubilation. Cole eventually realized that Hector and Elena were standing awkwardly near them, unsure of how to proceed.

"Everyone – these are the *amazing* people that have looked after me. This is Elena and Hector." Everyone shook hands.

"I'm Gabe. It's nice to...to meet..." His words caught in his throat and his eyes widened in shock.

"What is it?" Hector asked, chuckling nervously.

"Is your last name Aguilar?"

"Yes. How did you know?"

Tears welled in Gabe's eyes, and he wrapped his arms around Hector and pulled him in for a tight hug. Hector froze up.

"Gabe?" Cole asked in confusion.

Gabe seemed to come out of a trance. "Oh, I'm...I'm sorry. It's just that you, and your sister, remind me of some old friends that I used to have," he replied. He held a knowing expression on his smiling face.

"Well, thanks again for looking out for Cole. We really appreciate it," Brody said.

"Not a problem," Elena replied. She took a deep drag from her cigarette.

A Pinkerton agent stepped forward. "Sorry to interrupt, but we've got injured folks in the hacienda that need to be taken care of. The place is a real mess, too."

"You're right, we have a lot of work to do. Well, I guess this is goodbye," Hector said.

"Take care of yourselves," Cole said.

They turned around and headed to the horses that Gabe and Brody had used to get there.

"What a beautiful city! It's lucky that you didn't end up in Antarctica or something," Brody said. "Isn't it strange to think that all of this will radically change in just a few short years?"

"What do you mean?" Cole asked.

"Well, in about four years the President of Mexico will be forced to resign, the Mexican Revolution will break out, and Pancho Villa will rise to power. Mexico will look very different."

"How do you know so much about history?"

"I don't know!" Brody laughed. "Maybe it would've been a smarter idea to study history instead of acting. I'd definitely make more money."

Cole noticed the large smile on Gabe's face.

"What's that look for?"

"Well, you'd be happy, too, if you just met your great-great-grandfather and his sister!"

"What?! Who?"

"Hector and Elena! I recognized them immediately! Ever since abuela passed away, I've felt very far away from my family. In a strange way, it's almost like *The Astrolabe* knew that I needed to meet them. I will never forget this night."

Cole was bowled over by a sudden realization – Hector and Elena were in the photograph that was sitting next to Camila's hospital bed! He was shocked that he had never recognized them. He laughed at all the strange and wonderful ways that the universe worked, and they rode the horses back to the entrance to *The Astrolabe*.

CHAPTER TWENTY

Cole, Gabe, and Brody made their way onto *The Astrolabe* and settled into the front train compartment. They were all exhausted after the insane events of the past forty-eight hours. Cole ran to the train compartment that functioned as the kitchen and threw together a plate of turkey and cheese sandwiches. Then, they all sat down next to the main controls and dug into their food.

"Well, I know you're going to hate me for saying this, but we need to start thinking of a plan for when we get to London," Brody said. "It should only take us about thirty minutes to get there."

"Um...actually, Brody, can I talk to Gabe in private? It'll only take a second," Cole said. Gabe raised his eyebrows in surprise, but he didn't say anything.

Brody smirked. "Sure. Take your time, boys."

Cole blushed deeply, punched Brody on his arm, and left with Gabe.

"Where are we going?" Gabe asked eagerly. He smiled and followed Cole into an empty train compartment.

"I really wanted to talk to you about something," Cole said. His whole body was tingling with adrenaline, and he couldn't wait to get the words out of his mouth. "So...do you remember what you asked me at the Senior Ball? The question about moving in together?"

Gabe furrowed his brow in confusion. "Y-Yes. Why? I mean, you were pretty clear --"

"Forget everything that I said!" Cole blurted out. He grabbed Gabe's muscular shoulders and pulled him closer. "I know that I said I needed to think about it, and I'm sorry. I was just being an idiot."

"You're not an idiot --"

"I was scared and not thinking clearly. What if I mess things up between us after we move in? Or, what if we end up annoying each other?"

"Well, I'm sure that will happen at some point!" Gabe laughed.

"But I'm not worried about that anymore. I want to be with you, whatever the situation is. Good or bad. When I was in Mexico and I didn't know whether I would make it through the day or not, the one thing that kept me going was the thought of you. You mean everything to me. So, what am I waiting for?!"

A big smile lit up Gabe's face, the smile that made Cole dizzy, and he looked warmly down into Cole's eyes. "Do you mean that? You really want to move in together?"

"I mean it." Cole stood on his tip toes and pulled Gabe into a deep kiss. Gabe broke away for a second and pressed Cole against the door to the train compartment, a hungry look in his eyes. Then, they resumed kissing and their bodies melted into each other.

*****

Ten minutes later, the boys walked back into the front compartment looking slightly disheveled. Brody was surrounded by stacks of books. He looked up and smiled wryly.

"Well. You've been gone for a while."

Cole and Gabe blushed deeply. "I don't know what you're talking about," Cole said.

"*Anyway*," Brody said. "While you were in Mexico City, I pulled some books from the library that will help us navigate Victorian London and locate Jaxon. I don't have as much information as I'd like, but there's enough to get us going." He opened a heavy, leather-bound book and flipped through the pages until he found the one that he was looking for. "So. Here's what we know: Jaxon murdered Oscar Wilde shortly before his trial on April 26th, 1895. The trial was at the Old Bailey Courthouse in London. So, we need to head there when we arrive."

"I guess they have, like, horse-drawn carriages that we can take?" Cole asked.

"Unfortunately, yes. Not too different from 1907. So, it might take us some time to get the courthouse."

"So...we go to the Old Bailey and then what? Stop Jaxon?" Gabe asked.

"Yes, but there's a second part to this plan. According to history books now, Oscar's famous mechanical sketches suddenly disappeared before his trial. We all know that's a lie, so Jaxon must've destroyed them before he murdered Oscar. They were last seen with Lillie Langtry," Brody explained. "We'll need to find a way to get those sketches and keep them safe from Jaxon, before figuring out a way to sneak into the courthouse. It's a lot, I know, but maybe Lillie Langtry can help!"

"Who is Lillie Langtry?" Cole asked.

Brody rolled his eyes. "Ugh. Cole! You need to know these things! Lillie Langtry was a famous socialite and actress. She basically ruled London in the 1890's. Super gorgeous. She was also a good friend of Oscar Wilde's. After he died, she saved his mechanical drawings and gave them to the British Museum. As we all know, engineers later took the drawings and used them as inspiration for the first mechanical designs."

"Well, that sounds like as good a plan as any," Gabe said.

"So...yeah! We'll track down Lillie Langtry and then we'll, um, take care of Jaxon. Sound good?"

A heavy silence fell over the group. They all knew what "take care of Jaxon" meant, but none of them wanted to verbalize that brutal truth. Whatever happened, it was going to be a difficult decision.

"Well...we can always figure out how we're going to, um, apprehend Jaxon when we get to London, I guess," Cole said.

"What about disguises?" Gabe asked. "It'll be easier to blend into the city that way."

"Ooh great idea!" Brody cried. "Let's look through the costume compartment!"

They walked down the hallway, passing by the dozens of different train cars, before they arrived at the costume train compartment and walked inside. Long rows of clothing racks stretched out in front of them, laden with coats, dresses, pants, and suits. Every type of fabric, in every color, was represented. Arthur had spent the past two years scouring every thrift store in Mechanica City to stock the costume compartment.

The boys walked down the long aisles and dug through the racks, passing through hundreds of years of fashion history in minutes. Ten minutes later, Gabe, Cole, and Brody compared their disguises: Brody wore a top hat, a black suit, and held a glossy cane; Gabe had chosen a long waistcoat with a matching four-piece suit; Cole put on a wool vest, brown slacks, and a newsboy cap.

"This isn't too bad," Gabe said. "This is actually pretty close to what we usually wear."

"I grabbed a fistful of Victorian English pounds and shillings that we can use in an emergency," Brody said. "No one will be able to tell that they're fakes."

As soon as they walked back into the front train compartment, a series of loud *thumps* filled the room. Gabe moved the window curtains aside and saw a random assortment of objects floating by in the air. The objects, all from the 1890's, included a kinetograph, a flock of fluttering Victorian novels like *The Awakening* by Kate Chopin and *Dracula* by Bram Stoker, a statue of Queen Victoria that spun lazily by itself, and a crowd of steel workers that were fighting men in suits.

"It looks like we're getting close," Cole said.

"Despite the circumstances, I'm really excited to visit Victorian London!" Brody said. "I hope that we get a chance to talk to Oscar. I'd love to pick his brain and learn about his creative process. He *is* iconic, after all."

Something large and heavy suddenly struck the side of the train. The table that they were sitting at shifted and slid across the floor. Cole, Gabe, and Brody jumped out of their seats in shock.

"What was that?" Gabe asked.

"What now?" Cole groaned. He peered out of the window and immediately reared back in shock; what he saw sent a chill down his spine. Floating alongside the train was something out of a nightmare. A colossal, translucent creature, roughly the size of a small whale, was swimming by the floating 1890's detritus. Wickedly sharp spikes ran down the length of the monster's long back, and its mouth, or what Cole assumed was its mouth, was a gaping hole that was lined with sharp, jagged teeth.

"What...what the hell is that thing?" Brody whispered.

Cole's voice trembled. "I...I don't know what it's called. I've always called it a Time Beast. This is the thing that went inside Malick and possessed him all those years ago. But I...I destroyed it..."

The Time Beast suddenly shifted to the left and slammed its body into the side of *The Astrolabe* again. The front train compartment, along with the rest of the train, began to violently shake back and forth. Gabe, Cole, and Brody were thrown into a wall.

"We have to stop it!" Brody yelled.

"Wait here!" Cole replied. With blood pounding in his ears, he ran out of the train compartment and raced to the armory. Five minutes later, he returned, out of breath, with three heavy blasters in his hands.

"Let's smash the window and shoot it down!" Brody cried.

A bone-shaking roar reverberated from outside the window and the floating monster slammed into the train once again – they were running out of time.

"Hold on!" Cole said. He used the butt of his blaster to smash the window and the glass shattered. A strong gust of wind poured in and chairs and books were lifted off the floor and sucked outside.

"Watch out!" Brody shouted. He aimed and fired his blaster. A neon green energy blast exploded from the gun barrel and struck the Time Beast's face. It opened its slimy maw and roared in pain, but, to Brody's disappointment, it continued to chase after them.

"Approaching destination," an automated voice said over the intercom.

"As soon as we get out at the Decade Station, that thing will attack us!" Gabe cried. He aimed and fired at the translucent beast, but it moved out of the way of the energy blast.

"I can't get a good enough angle!" Cole said, gritting his teeth in frustration. His hands started shaking, but he forced himself to focus. "I've got to get closer. Gabe, stay here and keep shooting. Brody and I will get to a higher location and hit it from there!"

"Why do I have to go with you?" Brody complained.

"Let's go!" Cole opened up a hatch in the ceiling and scrambled up and out, Brody begrudgingly following behind.

"Be careful!" Gabe said.

A harsh wind whipped their clothes as they stepped out onto the roof of *The Astrolabe*. Cole was very aware of the placement of his feet this time – he wasn't going to fall off again.

"Look out!" Brody screamed. The two boys hit the floor as the Time Beast flew by, jaws wide, and soared over them.

"Screw you, you bastard!" Cole screamed over the wind, and he and Brody began to fire off blast after blast at the lumbering behemoth. The energy blasts struck the creature in the face, on its underbelly, and down the length of its back, leaving burning holes in its flesh. It howled in anguish and a green liquid poured out of the bullet holes.

"I think it's working! Keep going!" Cole yelled. In the distance he could see the 1890's Decade Station quickly approaching.

A panicked scream erupted from below. Cole looked over the edge of the roof and his blood went cold: the Time Beast was hovering in front of the window, floating in place like a great white shark, and it was doing everything it could to possess Gabe.

"GABEEEEEE!" he bellowed.

Cole and Brody ran down the length of the train roof and slid through the hatch. They found Gabe standing in the middle of the compartment, frozen in place, and he was leaning back at a strange angle as the horrifying beast was forcing its way inside his mouth. Cole screamed and opened fire on the beast, hitting it over and over with energy blasts. Green blood splattered the walls. Gabe choked and gagged as the wounded creature backed out of his mouth; it roared in their faces and flew out of the window. Then, Gabe collapsed to the ground.

With a final unearthly shriek of pain, the menacing Time Beast, blood pouring out of its stomach like a waterfall, turned a dark gray color and died. Its limp corpse floated in place, unseeing white eyes staring straight ahead.

An enormous wave of relief washed over Cole, but there was no time to relax just yet – Gabe was hurt.

"Gabe, wake up! Are you OK?" he yelled. He grabbed his boyfriend by the shoulders and shook him roughly. "Wake up!"

Gabe came to with a start and looked around. "Wh-What happened? Are we safe? Where is that thing?"

"It's gone! We took care of it!" Cole explained. He hugged him tightly and helped him to his feet. "Don't worry, we're safe."

"Well...safe for now," Brody said. "We're approaching the 1890's Decade Station and it looks like we have company."

A thick plume of smoke was belched out of the chimney as *The Astrolabe* slowed down and came to a halt in front of the Decade Station. Cole, Gabe, and Brody held their breaths as they moved to the window and peered outside. A Project Hominum member holding a large rifle was pacing angrily back and forth on the white, wooden platform. He paused and pointed his gun at the train when it stopped, but, when no one came out, he went back to pacing and screaming into a handheld receiver.

"JAXON, ANSWER ME!" he barked. He pulled at his hair in frustration. "You were supposed to pick me up *48 hours ago*! I have done EVERYTHING THAT YOU HAVE ASKED! TELL ME WHAT TO DO!"

Cole looked at Brody and Gabe. "Do you think there are more guards around?"

"It looks like it's just him," Gabe answered.

"Perfect." Cole slipped on the Invisibility Vambrace and slid open the train door.

"Who's there?!" the guard yelled. He whipped his gun around and pointed it at the open door. Without a sound, Cole slowly tiptoed across the platform and moved behind him.

"I know someone is ther--"

Before he could finish his sentence, the guard's eyes rolled into the back of his head and he collapsed to the ground. Cole materialized behind him.

"Man, this is useful!"

Brody and Gabe ran onto the platform and they all stood in front of the Time Screen.

"We finally made it! Are we ready for this?" Brody asked. Cole and Gabe nodded. Then, Brody typed in April 25th, 1895, London, England" and a wormhole folded open in front of them. They ran and jumped through it.

CHAPTER TWENTY-ONE

A second wormhole materialized inside a large, marble fountain. Brody, Gabe, and Cole tumbled out, rolled through a hole that was in the center of the fountain, and landed on the cold floor; the hole closed with a popping sound. The boys slowly looked up and noticed a small crowd of people standing around them. They were all wearing dark and stuffy clothing, as well as similar expressions of shock on their faces.

"Um. He-Hello! Does anyone know where we can find a taxi?" Brody asked.

There was a high-pitched shriek in response and the crowd panicked and scattered in all directions. Women in corsets and long dresses ran screaming past them as Cole, Brody, and Gabe ran and hid behind a white, marble statue.

"What is this place?" Brody whispered.

Cole cautiously looked out from behind the tall statue and finally took in their surroundings: they were inside an immense hall that had been constructed entirely out of sheets of glass and cast iron. Scattered throughout the echoing chamber were sumptuous displays of artistry, such as rows of more marble statues, a long reflecting pool with large lily pads, and a large elm tree that grew out of the floor, its thick branches nearly touching the roof. Several feet above the floor was a long, wooden platform that was held up by intricate metal scaffolding draped with colorful flags; this makeshift second floor wound its way around the entire room. Cole looked up and gazed upon an impressive barrel-vaulted ceiling.

"It looks we're in some kind of museum. I think?" he finally said. "There has to be an exit around here somewhere."

When the pandemonium finally died down inside the hall, the boys moved out from behind the white statue and went looking for an exit.

Ten minutes later, after walking down crowded hallways that held large dinosaur sculptures, more fountains, and exhibitions of fruit, they finally located a glass door that led outside and they exited the massive building. Directly in front of them were several wide dirt paths that were bordered by large fountains spewing water. The night sky, dotted with bright stars, churned and roiled above them.

Cole spotted a line of black horse-drawn carriages standing in a row off in the distance, so the three boys ran over to the closest one.

"'Ello, gentlemen!" said a rosy-cheeked man sitting at the top of a Brougham carriage. He possessed a thick Cockney accent, and he wore a top hat, a long coat, as well as a wide smile on his face. Two brown horses were hitched to the carriage.

"Hello, sir. Could you tell us what this place is?" Cole asked.

"Ah ha! Lost your way, have you? Well, gentlemen, the building that stands before you is the famous Crystal Palace! Built in 1851 by Joseph Paxton for the Great Exhibition, the Crystal Palace is 564.18 meters long with an interior height of 39.01 meters."

"Can you take us to the Cadogan Hotel?" Brody asked.

"I would be happy to! The Cadogan Hotel, opened in 1887, is one of our city's finest luxury hotels. It's located in Chelsea. If you're lucky, you might catch a glimpse of the actress Lillie Langtry!"

A sharp current of excitement passed between the boys at the mention of Lillie Langtry's name.

"Wow, you really know a lot about this city!" Gabe said.

"I should 'ope so! Lived here all my life. Now, come on, lads. Let's get you to that hotel."

The three boys piled into the carriage and they took off down the dirt path. For the next hour and a half, the horses led them down wide, cobblestone streets while they listened to the driver, whose name was Rupert, rattle off an endless list of facts about the surrounding area. Cole tried his best to listen, but it was very difficult – the distinguished beauty of London was overwhelming and distracting. A cool night breeze tousled his hair and cleared his head as he stared out the window. After all the chaos of the past few days, it was so nice to be able to relax in his seat and enjoy the lush scenery. His eyes passed over patches of bright green trees and sloping, manicured lawns with gurgling streams winding through them.

Midway through their journey, dense forests and foliage thinned out and opened onto the quaint city district of Peckham. The carriage drove by long rows of small brick houses that stood next to tiny shops, as well as crowded fish and meat markets.

"'Peckham' is a Saxon name that means 'the village of the River Peck.' The river was a small stream that ran through this district until it was enclosed in 1823," Rupert explained. "On your left you will see the Peckham Rye railway station which opened in 1865. Thanks to the railway, quite a few workers from the inner city were able to sell their products out here. Very good for business!"

Cole's eyes widened in shock when they passed by a square building called The Museum of Firearms.

Brody bent down and picked up a newspaper that was lying on the floor of the carriage. As soon as he opened the paper up, he gasped loudly.

"What is it?" Cole asked.

"The...the date! I got it wrong!" he groaned. As Brody put his head in his hands, Cole grabbed the newspaper and looked at the date: April 25th, 1895.

"We're a day early..." Brody lamented.

"Everything all right back there?" Rupert asked.

"Everything's fine!" Cole yelled back. He turned and whispered to Brody, "It's OK, don't beat yourself up. We're here, so we'll just have to make it work. An extra day to settle our plans isn't such a bad thing."

As the carriage trundled through South London and finally into Chelsea, the streets became crowded with carriages and their surroundings took on a more refined and metropolitan look. A stately form of chaos flashed by Cole as the carriage sped on: muddy cobblestone streets that were bordered by row after row of red brick terraced houses; dark and smelly alleyways where homeless families slept on the filthy ground; wooden omnibuses occupied by women wearing hoop skirts and frilly bonnets; jagged, rusty factories off in the distance that spewed thick smoke into the air. Cole felt a strange sense of déjà vu, like he was looking around at Mechanica City, but through a kaleidoscope.

The carriage finally rolled to a stop in front of a five-story stone and brick building that stood on the corner of Pont Street. The Cadogan Hotel held a strong air of stately grandeur, with twin columns flanking the front entrance. Carefully tended flower pots rested in front of the windows. The hotel was pushed right up against a line of red brick apartment buildings with pointed roofs.

"Here you are!" Rupert said, tipping his top hat. "Enjoy your stay in London!" The three boys climbed out of the carriage, gave Rupert a tip, and he drove away.

"Well, we made it. A day early, but we made it. So, let's go and get those sketches from Lillie," Brody said. "She lives in room 109. Listen -- if anyone tries to stop us, we'll just tell them that we're producers who want to discuss a new project for her, OK?" Gabe and Cole nodded, and they walked through a pair of black double doors.

The main lobby was surprisingly small and intimate, yet it still radiated a sense of luxury. Groups of attractive men and women, dressed in white bow ties and wide-brimmed hats, sat on plush couches and chatted happily. Through a glass door, Cole could see a bar at the back of the room where more beautiful and wealthy guests were carousing.

A white-haired man in a black suit stood behind a lectern in front of a short staircase. Cole, Gabe, and Brody moved for the wooden staircase but were quickly stopped.

"Excuse me, gentleman. How may I assist you?" the concierge asked.

"We're just here to see Miss Langtry," Cole replied. He made for the stairs again, but the concierge stood in his way once more.

"Miss Langtry sees guests on an appointment basis only," he responded haughtily. "If you would like to go upstairs, then you will need to reserve a room."

"Let me handle this," Brody whispered to Cole and Gabe. He puffed out his chest and stepped forward, doing his best to appear in charge. "We're three theatre producers. We work for, um, Bennett, Hernandez, and Kim Associates and we're here to discuss a wonderful new opportunity for Miss Langtry. It's quite urgent."

"Well, Miss Langtry always informs me of guests that she's expecting ahead of time. I was not informed of this," the concierge said with a clipped tone. He was getting impatient.

Gabe suddenly had an idea. "Excuse me, sir. Listen – we *really* need to speak with Miss Langtry. Will this change your mind?" He surreptitiously pulled out a wad of bills from his pocket and placed them in the concierge's hand. The old man paused and stared at the money quizzically. Then, a large smile lit up his face.

"Many thanks, sir. You may go upstairs."

Cole and Brody stared at Gabe in surprise, but they stayed quiet and made their way up the wooden staircase.

They climbed to the second floor and came upon a long, carpeted hallway. Several white doors stood on each side of the hallway, and everything was bathed in warm, orange lantern light. The door to Lillie Langtry's apartment stood at the end of the hall.

"How did you know to offer him money?" Brody asked.

"I've seen people do it in movies. Everybody likes money!" Gabe laughed.

As they approached Lillie's apartment, a handsome man with greased hair and a thin moustache suddenly stepped out of the room. He stared at Brody, Gabe, and Cole in surprise as they approached. Then, he blushed deeply and hurried away from them as fast as he could.

Cole walked up to the door and knocked.

"Now, Howard! *Please*! You know that I have an event that I need to get to!" said a high-pitched, snobbish voice. The door opened and there stood Lillie Langtry. She had curly auburn hair and a pale, delicate face. A haughty glamour seemed to reflexively pour off her. She was wearing a corset and a heavy tea gown that had been made from bolts of a sumptuous lilac satin.

"Miss Langtry, we have to speak to you!" Brody said. "It's an emergency."

Lillie scowled and looked at him like he had just spoken gibberish. "Who are you? I've never seen you before in my life."

Without waiting for an answer, Brody shoved past her and pushed his way into the room. Gabe and Cole followed him and shut the door.

"What the *devil* do you think you're doing?!" Lillie shrieked. "Get out of my flat at once!"

"I know that this looks really strange, but we have to talk to you about something *extremely* important," Cole urged. "It has to do with Oscar Wilde." He took a moment to observe his cushy surroundings: warm, floral wallpaper covering the walls; an ornate fireplace with a large, ornamental mirror hanging above it; a white, decorative ceiling; mahogany cabinets that held many hand-painted vases.

A wry smile slowly crept up Lillie's face. "Ah. I *see*." She sauntered over to the chaise lounge and sat down. "Well, I'm afraid that I won't be able to get you any money from Oscar. As I'm sure you've heard, he's currently dealing with some legal issues. Poor soul."

"Money? We're not here for money," Gabe said.

Lillie furrowed her brow in confusion. "You're not prostitutes?"

Cole, Brody, and Gabe looked at each other and then burst out laughing.

"*No*, we're not prostitutes! But we desperately need your help. We're looking for a series of drawings. Oscar, um, told us that he left them with you."

Lillie's angular face blanched and she suddenly looked nervous. "D-Drawings? What on earth are you --"

"*Drawings of a human made out of metal!*" Brody interrupted. "Sketches on a piece of paper. *Please.* We know that you have them."

Lillie Langtry sprang to her feet in a rage, rising to her full height with hands on her

233

hips. "Now, you listen to me, young man – I don't know who you think you are, barging into my flat like this, but Lillie Langtry does not tolerate this!"

"Listen, a stranger is going to break into your apartment tonight and steal the sketches, so you need to give them to –"

"I don't know what sketches you're talking about, so get out before I call the police! Or maybe I'll scream!" She marched to the door and threw it open, motioning for them to leave.

"*FINE*! We're from the future!" Brody blurted out. He slammed the door shut and Lillie stepped back in shock.

"Wh-What did you just say?!"

"We're from the future. I know that it sounds crazy, but you have to believe me. We're here because we're trying to save Oscar!"

"But I *don't* believe you! That's preposterous! Now, you better leave, or --"

Brody suddenly pulled out his cell phone and held it up to her. He swiped his finger across the glass surface and opened the main screen. "Look. Do you see this? This is a cell phone. Have you ever seen anything like this before?"

Lillie took the phone and held it gingerly in her hands, inspecting every inch of it, her eyes wide with shock and awe. She moved back to the chaise lounge and slowly sat down, looking dazed.

"This is a lot to take in. I'm sorry that we have to involve you in this," Gabe said.

"But what you're saying is madness. I mean...*utter madness!* Time travel? You're off your head!"

"We know," Cole agreed.

"However...this device with the flickering images is certainly convincing. I'm going to need some strong tea for this conversation." She stood up and disappeared into the kitchen. The boys followed her.

Cole felt a painful sting of anxiety in his chest. They would have to deal with this situation delicately. They couldn't reveal too much about the future or it could have devastating consequences.

"Is Oscar's life in danger?" Lillie asked. She put a brass kettle on the stove.

"I'm afraid so. If we don't intervene, Oscar will be murdered before his trial tomorrow," Cole explained.

Lillie grabbed a paper fan from a side table and waved it dramatically in front of her face. "*M-Murdered*? Oh dear. Oh dear! That...That can't be right! Why would someone want to murder him? His writings are a bit risqué, and he's a bit of a dandy, but that's no reason to murder someone! What is so special about his sketches?"

"Well...we can't really tell you that. It's complicated," Brody admitted.

"You expect me to trust you, yet you won't tell me a bloody thing?"

Brody stepped to the front of the group and said, "We don't have all night, OK? Don't believe us? Well, how about this -- Arthur Jones is the father of your daughter!"

Lillie's mouth fell open and she gasped; her fan fell to the floor. "How...How do you know that? *That is my personal business!*"

"We told you -- we're from the future. That information is in history books. So – will you help us?"

Lillie stared around at them in muted horror. She was so shocked that she couldn't speak.

"Hold on...you said that you read about it in books?" she finally said after a few seconds. "My personal life is in *history books?*"

"Of course. You're famous in our world!"

A big smile suddenly lit up Lillie's pale face and her high cheekbones flushed. Tears filled her eyes.

"Really?" she cooed. "Well, I won't say that I'm surprised by this news. I happen to be very aware of my talents. But flattery will certainly get you everywhere, so, which of my performances is your favorite?"

"Oh, ummm..." Brody mumbled. "I mean, we've read so much about your plays..."

"Yes?"

"Apparently you were really good in that, um, that one Shakespeare show --"

"Ah yes, Macbeth! One of my favorite productions! My Lady Macbeth was *very* well received. Well, I guess I can't say no to my avid admirers, now, can I? Let me get those sketches for you." She swept out of the room, briefly leaving the boys alone, before returning with a small stack of papers in one arm and a tea tray in the other. They moved to drink their tea at the kitchen table and examined the drawings.

"I can't believe that these doodles are so important. Aren't they adorable? Oh, Oscar. Can you really ensure that nothing bad happens to him? We aren't exactly speaking at the moment, as his personal choices leave *much* to be desired, but I certainly don't want him hurt."

"We can," Cole assured her. "But we'll need your help. Can you sneak us into Oscar's trial tomorrow? You *are* famous, after all."

The fire seemed to extinguish in Lillie's eyes and she shook her head. "Oh, *no*. No, no, no! That's *quite* impossible. You see, I may have made a name for myself, but that means little when it comes to the justice system. However, I do know someone who may be able to assist you."

"Who?" Gabe asked.

"A man named Lord Alfred Douglas. It would actually be more -- "

Brody groaned.

"Excuse me?" Lillie said.

"Oh! Sorry. I just...um...I'm *really* not a fan."

"Most people aren't," Lillie quipped.

"But he *would* be a great source of help. How can we meet him?"

Lillie walked over and absentmindedly put her fingers inside a large bird cage hanging by the window. The puffed finch sitting inside nuzzled her finger. "Well...it just so happens that I'm going to a party tonight and Lord Alfred Douglas will be there. If you promise not to cause trouble, you may escort me."

Cole's face lit up. "That's perfect! When can we leave?"

"Now! Follow me!" Lillie swept out of her apartment, the three boys in tow.

CHAPTER TWENTY-TWO

"Ease up a bit, Jasper! I'd like to make it to the party in one piece!" Lillie reprimanded. The horse-drawn carriage that they were sitting in shook from side to side as they dodged traffic.

"Sorry, miss!" her driver exclaimed. They were speeding down Piccadilly Street, through a lively section of the city that was called Piccadilly Circus. The glowing moon hung above the lines of row houses and hotels that rose up every few feet, with their white exteriors and numerous chimneys. Cole 's eyes feasted on the visuals that flashed by his window: the London Pavilion, its refined post and lintel exterior and rows of columns, and the Criterion Theatre, alluring and bathed in yellow light from nearby gas lampposts. Each of these ornate limestone structures surrounded a large bronze fountain called the Shaftesbury Memorial Fountain. A winged statue topped the fountain, the Greek god Anteros.

The carriage made a wide turn onto Regent Street, and the row houses bent with the curve of the road.

"So. Where is this party?" Brody asked.

"The Albemarle Club. Very exclusive, but they'll let you in since you're with me. You've heard of it, I'm sure."

"Uh, no, actually," Cole admitted.

"What?! Does it not exist in your time?"

"No, it doesn't," Brody said.

"Oh! How disappointing. Well, I suppose I ought to enjoy every moment of it while I still can. We shall arrive shortly."

Moments later, the driver slowed the carriage to a stop in front of a luxurious stone edifice that had an iron balcony resting above the arched entrance. They stepped out, stood on the sidewalk, and Cole looked around at the metropolis that surrounded him; he felt like he had been dropped into a crowded stone maze. Men and women rushed by him on the sidewalk.

"Miss Langtry! Miss Langtry, wait!"

They all turned around and saw the white-haired concierge from earlier running toward them in a panic.

"What is it, Basil?" Lillie asked. "You look like you've seen a ghost!"

Basil doubled over and clutched at the stitch in his side before answering. There was a deep cut on his forehead. *"Th-Three masked men just broke into your flat!* I tried to subdue them but...well...I'm sorry to say that they got the best of me..."

Lillie's eyes grew wide. "Good heavens! When did this happen?

"Just now. I got here as fast as I could!"

"Did they steal anything?"

"No, thankfully. They certainly made a mess in your flat, but everything remains. Apologies again, miss. The authorities have been informed."

Lille turned to the boys with a knowing look. "You were right," she whispered. She turned back to the concierge. "Don't worry, Basil. Thank you for telling me. Make sure that you have that cut looked at."

A doorman in a stiff suit opened the door for them and they walked into the club. A large group of men and women stared at them in excitement as they moved through the small space.

"Wow, do you know all these people?" Brody whispered.

"Of course, darling," Lillie responded. "Now, this is where I must leave you, I'm afraid. Mustn't keep my audience waiting. Good luck on your journey. I pray your plan to save Oscar is a successful one."

"Before you go, would you take the sketches?" Brody asked. He pulled them out of his jacket and passed them to her. "Now, this is very important – put these in a safety deposit box in the bank."

"They're safe with me."

"Thank you, Miss Langtry, for all of your help," Cole said.

"Of course. Oh, and one last thing: Lord Alfred is that young man in the corner with the blonde hair." She beamed at them with a dazzling smile, turned around, and moved to greet the rest of the people in the room.

"How are we going to convince this Lord Alfred Douglas guy to sneak us into the trial tomorrow?" Gabe asked.

"Well, we know that, historically, his weaknesses are gifts, his narcissism, and money," Brody replied. "Oh, and men. We'll have to think of a way to take advantage of those weaknesses somehow."

"That seems a bit cruel, though. Right?" Cole asked.

"Yeah, probably. But Ruby needs our help. We've got a job to do," Brody said. "Besides, Alfred was pretty cruel in his lifetime. All bets are off."

Brody led them over to the blonde boy in the corner. He was surrounded by a group of attractive young men wearing four-piece suits.

"Lord Alfred Douglas!" Brody cried, holding out his hand. "Lovely to meet you. My name is, um, Ogbert Covington. These are my friends, um..."

"Barnaby and Crispin," Gabe finished for him.

Lord Alfred slowly turned his head and stared at Brody, irritation written all over his sour face. He was very thin, with skin the color of curdled milk and a large nose. His heavily lidded eyes looked Brody up and down dismissively.

"Ah, yes. I saw you arrive with Lillie. Friends of hers?"

"Great friends! We've, um, acted with her before," Cole said.

"So...what do you want?" he asked. The group of men standing around him snickered.

"Oh. Um, well...I was hoping that we could talk to you about Oscar Wilde. We have some, um, information that I think you'll be interested in," Brody said.

"Is that right?"

"Um...yes?"

"Well, that's interesting, since I know everything there is to know about Oscar. In fact, I highly doubt that there is anyone who knows him better than I. Now, I'm trying to enjoy my drink. Please leave." Albert and his group of friends turned their backs and moved to another side of the room.

"What do we do now?" Gabe whispered.

Cole's spirits sank like a heavy stone as they walked away. *Well...this is never going to work...*

Brody puffed out his chest, steadied himself, and moved over to Lord Alfred again. He grabbed him by the arm.

"Excuse me, but this is impor --"

"How *dare* you! Get your hands off me!" Lord Alfred shouted as he whirled around.

Brody held up his hands in surrender and plastered a wide smile on his face. "Easy, *easy*. So, listen – I lied! The real reason that I'm here is because I *had* to meet you."

"And why is that?"

"Because...well, are you really going to make me say it in front of all these people?"

Cole and Gabe looked at each other in confusion. They waited anxiously for what would happen next.

"Speak now or I'll have you thrown out of this building," Lord Alfred growled.

"I want to spend some time with you. Some, uh, *alone time*, if my meaning is clear. I think you're gorgeous." He pulled out a wad of cash from his pocket and held it up.

Lord Alfred scoffed, but a small smile crept up his thin mouth. "Is that so?"

"You're also a *much* better writer than Oscar."

Alfred's eyes lit up. The group of men around him gasped.

"Well well *well*. How enchanting," Lord Alfred purred. "You're quite forward, aren't you? I like that. How about we discuss this further in a private room upstairs? Second floor?" He linked his arm with Brody's and led him out of the room. Brody shot Gabe and Cole a surprised look as he left.

"Bloody hell. He's *always* doing this," one of Lord Alfred's friends grumbled. "Leave some for the rest of us."

For the next several minutes, Gabe and Cole stood in uncomfortable silence while the crowd around them drank and made small talk. Brody hadn't mentioned where he was going, so they felt lost. However, without any other instructions, they slipped out of the room and headed upstairs to the second floor. They made their way down a quiet hallway.

"Brody? Brody?" Cole whispered. Brody suddenly stepped out of a door and waved them inside a bedroom. When they entered the room, they were shocked to see Lord Alfred Douglas cowering in the corner. Brody was pointing his blaster at him.

"What the hell are you doing?!" Cole yelled.

"What? I had to think of some way to keep him here!" Brody replied.

"Please help me!" Lord Alfred cried. "This man has gone mad!"

Cole shut the door and stood in front of it.

"Then...Then you're in on this, too! The lot of you! Do you have any idea who you're messing with? When my father hears about --"

"Your father can't stand you. What is he going to do?" Brody scoffed.

Lord Alfred's lip curled and his face flushed red. "How *dare* you! HEEELLLLPPPP! SOMEONE HELP MEEEE!!!!!"

Cole ran to him and covered his mouth with his hand. "*Shut up!* Scream again and we'll put a gag over your mouth. Understand?"

Lord Alfred nodded his head and Cole removed his hand from his mouth. "Wh-What do you want from me?!"

"We need you to get us into Oscar's trial tomorrow. He's in danger."

Lord Alfred scoffed. "Danger? Impossible. He is sitting in a jail cell right now that is surrounded by guards. I visited yesterday."

"Well, it's a bit complicated," Brody said.

Alfred crossed his arms and glared at them. "Why do you care so much about Oscar, anyway? Let me guess – he paid you for sex and now you want more money?"

"Why does everyone think that we're prostitutes?" Gabe said to Cole.

"Well, I'm sorry to disappoint you, but Oscar doesn't have any money to give. As I said before, he's in a jail cell. Besides, he is in love with me. Not any of you. We don't want or need your help," Lord Alfred said smugly.

"Oh please," Brody growled. "You're leaving for France! Escaping and leaving Oscar to deal with this on his own."

Lord Alfred's face fell. "How...How did you know that?"

"It doesn't matter!" Brody roared. "You know what? I'm sorry, but I need to say something."

"Be careful..." Cole warned.

"Let's be honest – you're partially the reason why Oscar's in trouble with the law to begin with! You convinced him to sue your father, and look where you are now! And you have the *audacity* to --"

"Well, I'm not the only one who is leaving!" Lord Alfred cried. He sat down on a bed and put his head in his hands. "And Oscar told me to go to Paris! He begged me to go! How dare you judge me. Who do you think you are, you vicious cad!" Bitter tears of anger began to pour down his cheeks and he sobbed loudly. "You sit there and call me selfish? Selfish, indeed! My father is a horrible, sick man. My brother Francis took his own life because of his cruelty! You have no bloody idea what I've been through. I told Oscar to press charges because I wanted my father rotting in a jail cell. That way, he couldn't bother us anymore! I was doing the right thing!"

A blotchy red hue burned on Brody's cheeks. His hands were shaking. "Well, all of that may be true, but you still treated Oscar terribly. In fact, you treat *everyone* terribly! You spent all his money, you cheated on him all the time. Your parents should've given you a swift kick in the pants when you were a child. Maybe you wouldn't have grown up to be such a pompous bastard."

"A *bastard*?! *How dare you!* Your ignorance is astounding." Lord Alfred burst into tears again and sobbed louder. "Why are you doing this to me? How...How do you know all of this?!"

"Brody, that's enough!" Cole yelled. The room fell silent. He pulled Brody aside and whispered, "You need to let it go, OK? We're wasting time now. Lord Alfred isn't going to change. No matter how much you scold him. We have to move on."

Brody stood there, his chest burning with anger, but he took a slow, deep breath and eventually nodded.

"Dammit. Y-You're right...I got carried away. I'm sorry. I don't even know what I'm saying anymore. This is *really* difficult, Cole. Knowing what's going to happen in the future. I...I don't think that I can do this anymore." He turned away from them and stood by himself.

Cole walked over to the bed and sat next to Lord Alfred. "Listen...I'm really sorry about this. I am. My friend is, um, under a lot of stress. Big fan of Oscar. Anyway, here's the deal -- Oscar *really* is in danger. I can promise you that we wouldn't be here if that wasn't true. Now, I can't tell you anything specific, but he's going to be murdered tomorrow if you don't help us. You don't want that to happen, right? I know you don't. You love him."

Alfred moved towards the window and stared out of it, lost in thought. "I...I guess that I do. In my own way. I *am* his muse, after all. And, you know, I did want to give evidence in his case, but I wasn't allowed! I can't lose him. Who would murder him? That's abhorrent!"

"I'm sorry, but I can't tell you that. It will make things worse, trust me," Cole said. "But will you help us?"

Lord Alfred let out a long sigh and nodded his head. "Fine...I'll help you. It's not as if I have a choice in the matter. The guards know me at the jail, so they'll let you through. Now, will you *please* let me go?"

"Absolutely not. We can't," Brody said sternly. He held a troubled expression on his face. "He's just going to escape if we let him go!"

"But I believe you!" Lord Alfred whined. "Why would I run away?"

Cole's eyes flashed to Gabe for guidance. "Well...Brody's right," he finally said. "It's the only way to ensure that he doesn't screw up the mission."

Lord Alfred groaned and sat down on the bed again. "This is bloody ridiculous!"

Cole looked down at his wristwatch. It was just after midnight. "Well, the trial isn't for several more hours. What should we do until then?"

"We can just stay here and take turns sleeping. I could also *really* use a drink and some food," Brody answered. Cole was happy to see that some of his earlier tension appeared to have vanished.

"I agree. Since you're going to continue to keep me captive, you might as well give me something to drink. I'll take some wine. A lovely bottle of Chardonnay would suffice," Lord Alfred declared. Cole, Brody, and Gabe rolled their eyes.

Using the Invisibility Vambrace, Cole snuck down to the kitchen and brought back a large plate of finger sandwiches and a dusty bottle of wine (not Chardonnay, though, much to Lord Alfred's annoyance.) Then, for the rest of the night, they occupied themselves with their alcohol and snacks. The more wine that he drank, the looser Lord Alfred's tongue became, and he began to entertain them with bawdy tales about the people that ran London's nightlife as well as his life with Oscar. Despite his intense dislike of the blonde dandy, Brody couldn't help but get sucked into Lord Alfred's stories.

Late into the night, after everyone had finally fallen asleep, Cole stood in front of the window and looked down on the dark streets below. His mind churned and spun anxiously, flipping through multiple worst-case scenarios in an attempt to solve every possible obstacle. A big part of him knew that this was futile, but he had to occupy his mind somehow. Everything had to go perfectly.

Cole sighed deeply and lifted his eyes to the churning sky; it would be morning in a few hours. The time had come to save Ruby, restore Karma and the rest of the mechanicals, and set things right.

CHAPTER TWENTY-THREE

Cole jerked awake to a voice that said, "Alright, lads! It's almost time for the trial. Get me out of here *now*."

Lord Alfred wrenched the curtains open, allowing a steady beam of sunlight to come inside. Gabe, Brody, and Cole groaned as they slowly got to their feet, too exhausted to form words.

Thirty minutes later, a hansom cab dropped them off at the front of the Old Bailey. Cole looked up at the large and imperious courthouse and a chill ran down his spine. Thick walls of dreary, ominous stone made up the rectangular structure. As Cole's eyes passed over the building, he felt an undeniably magnetic quality exuding from it, as if he might get sucked inside if he stared for too long. If anything went wrong, would they be able to get out?

"Follow me," Lord Alfred demanded. "And don't say a word. I'll do the talking."

The three boys nodded and followed him to the front entrance, where a crowd of people were moving into the courthouse.

"All right James? Lovely weather we're having."

"Oy! What are you doin' 'ere?" a police officer barked. He was wearing a tall helmet and the strap rested under his prominent chin.

"My friends and I are here to see Mr. Wilde."

"Ohhh is that right, little dandy? Here to see your boyfriend, are ya? You two are disgusting."

"Yes, yes. You tell me that every time I come here."

"You know, I heard that he's finally going to trial today. Good riddance, I say."

The three boys glared at the police officer, anger bubbling in their stomachs, but Lord Alfred simply smiled and laughed.

"Oh, James. Always with your jokes. But anyway, please let us through."

"Absolutely not. Lettin' you in is one thing, and God knows I didn't want to do that, but a whole group of buggers? No."

"This is preposterous. Nothing untoward is going to happen. Obviously. You know, I don't think my father will appreciate the way that I'm being treated."

The police officer raised himself to his full height and glowered. "Now, you listen here -- I don't care what some invert's father has to say about anything. Tell him whatever you like, but you lot aren't getting inside."

Lord Alfred sighed, turned around, and looked into Cole's eyes. A look passed between them, one that was simultaneously mournful and determined.

"Protect him," Lord Alfred whispered. Then, he turned back around, held up his hand, and slapped the guard in the face.

Chaos broke out. The crowd that was standing in front of the entrance screamed and went running. The police officer hit Lord Alfred in the face and grabbed him by the wrists.

"RUN!" Lord Alfred yelled as he was dragged to the ground. The boys ran into the courthouse and passed through an open marble hall.

"Ugh! *So* happy to be away from him!" Brody said.

"You have to admit that he really helped us out, though!" Gabe replied.

"We're almost there," Cole said. "Let's finish this!"

They turned a corner and finally came upon the courtroom. A crowd was slowly making their way inside. Through the open door, Cole could see a large room that was packed with stuffy old men and women in dark clothes. They all held stern expressions on their faces.

"Where is Oscar? This is where he comes in, right?" Gabe asked. The three boys moved behind a stone pillar to hide.

"He gets stabbed to death right before the trial starts, so Jaxon has to be around here somewhere," Brody said. "Let's wait and see what happens. I can't believe we're about to see Oscar Wilde in person!"

They didn't have to wait very long, because a few minutes later, Jaxon turned a corner and walked down the hall. He was dressed in a dark police officer uniform; Oscar Wilde trailed behind him. A burst of white-hot rage coursed through Cole at the sight of this man, the one who had caused everyone so many problems.

"There he is! Any minute now..." Brody whispered.

Jaxon and Oscar paused in front of the court room door. They began to speak to each other, but none of the boys could hear what was said.

"Any minute now..."

Suddenly, Jaxon reached into his coat and pulled out a long knife. Before he even knew what he was doing, Cole jumped out from behind the pillar, held up his blaster, and pulled the trigger. The blast struck Jaxon's hand and knocked the knife onto the floor.

"DAMN YOU, YOU BASTARD!" Jaxon roared at Cole. Then, he turned and wrapped his large hands around Oscar's neck and squeezed.

Cole and Gabe ran and slammed Jaxon to the ground; Oscar broke away from Jaxon's grasp and stumbled into the wall. The two boys and Jaxon rolled around on the floor, kicking and punching.

Oscar's mouth fell open and he looked on in shock. "Th-Thank you. You saved me!"

Brody's heart soared and a wide smile stretched across his face. "No, *thank you*. Really. Your life and your artistry changed the world! Now, go!"

Oscar looked confused by Brody's kind words, but he nodded, ran into the courtroom, and bolted the door behind him – he was safe.

"Oof!" Gabe groaned loudly. Jaxon had found an opening and shoved his knee into his stomach.

As they all broke apart, gasping for air and sweating profusely, the air above them suddenly began to vibrate. A deafening roar filled their ears, and as they screamed, a bright flash of light filled the room and blinded them.

As soon as the rumbling stopped, Cole slowly raised his head and caught sight of Jaxon running down the hallway.

"We did it!" Brody said.

"We can't celebrate now! Follow him!" Cole cried. They all jumped to their feet and sprinted after Jaxon, streaking through the courthouse, nearly knocking several people out of the way. Cole ducked as an energy blast flew past his shoulder and slammed into the wall, but he kept running.

Jaxon barreled through the front entrance and exited the Old Bailey; the three boys stayed hot on his trail.

As they ran after him, a group of Project Hominum members emerged from the shadows and gave chase. Energy blasts went flying. The boys turned and fired their blasters, striking the terrorists and sending them toppling to the ground.

"Stop running, you stupid bastard!" Gabe yelled. He aimed and fired several shots at Jaxon's back, but each energy blast missed its target. Jaxon returned fire; the blasts slammed into a nearby lamppost.

"Out of the way!" Brody screamed as they ran down a crowded brick alleyway. Men and women screamed and jumped out of the way as they flew down the path.

An old stone clock tower loomed up ahead. Dodging in and out of horse-drawn carriages, Jaxon ran up the street, kicked open a door, and disappeared into the tower. Cole, severely out of breath, dug deep within himself and continued running.

They followed Jaxon up a narrow, wooden staircase. Up and up it went, all the way to the dizzying top.

Jaxon growled and fired off an energy blast; Brody cried out in surprise as the blast struck the wall next to him.

They clattered up the stairs and finally emerged at the top of the clock tower. Each of the four walls held a massive, circular sheet of glass, and inside the sheets of glass were long, black clock hands. Positioned in the middle of the room was a square turret clock.

Cole quickly glanced around the room. It looked like a group of people had been living here for several days; a number of sleeping bags had been rolled out, and piles of trash littered the wooden floors.

"There's nowhere else to go, Jaxon! It's over!" Brody yelled.

Jaxon backed into a corner and pointed his gun at them. He had a crazed smile and sweat poured down his face. Like a caught animal, he paced back and forth and clawed at the wall.

"Where is Ruby? Where is my sister?" Cole screamed.

"Come near me and I'll kill you!"

"I'm not going to ask you again – where the hell is my sister?" Cole demanded.

Jaxon lowered his blaster and released a slow, barking laugh. "So...*this* is how it all ends. I was so close. So close. But now, you'll just have to deal with the consequences. When every single human being has been replaced by filthy, disgusting robots...*then* you'll see."

"Nobody is getting 'replaced.' Mechanicals are *not* our enemy! They never have been. Your paranoia has done nothing but rot your mind. We're not going to let you hurt anyone else, Jaxon."

"Oh, is that right? You think that Project Hominum will end after this? I wouldn't be so sure about that. But, honestly, none of that matters anyway. I won't be around to see it. I'm getting out of this horrific world that refuses to save itself."

"Wait --" Brody said.

"HUMANS FIRST!" Jaxon bellowed. He put his gun into his mouth.

"NO!" Cole screamed.

Jaxon pulled the trigger and his head whipped back; thick, red blood splashed against the wall behind him. With a loud *thump*, his body crashed to the floor.

Everything seemed to slow down, as if Cole was watching a scene in slow motion. Shock and despair flooded his mind, and he felt like he was falling down a dark hole with no bottom in sight. He slowly collapsed to his knees, pounding the floor with his fists.

"No no no no *NO!*" he screamed. How were they supposed to find Ruby now? After everything that they had gone through, this couldn't be the end.

"Cole, come on. Don't...Don't do that. We'll figure something out, OK?" Gabe said. He kneeled down and wrapped his arms around Cole.

"Cole?" a voice said. Cole jumped to his feet and looked around. His heart was pounding in his chest.

"What was that?" Brody asked.

"Hello? Somebody help me out of here! Please, I'm stuck!"

The three boys moved around the clock tower, pressing and knocking on the stone walls. Cole's hand pressed on a loose stone and a panel slid open. A woman with a bruised face and ragged blonde hair tumbled out – it was Ruby.

"Thank you thank you thank you!" she sobbed. Cole hugged her tightly.

CHAPTER TWENTY-FOUR

As soon as they returned from *The Astrolabe,* Gabe and Cole left Ruby in Brody's care and flew the delivery dirigible to Wells Hospital. As they flew through the city, Cole noticed that the sky had returned to normal.

When they arrived, the hospital was fully up and running again. They found Arthur and Sabina waiting in the convalescence area. The room was now packed with mechanical and human nurses rushing from patient to patient, mending broken bones and treating head wounds; Cole's heart soared at the sight of the mechanical staff.

Sabina, Gabe, and Cole helped Arthur, now in a thick cast, get into the dirigible and they flew back home.

They were greeted by a loud scream when they returned; Karma was standing in front of the door, waiting for them. Cole jumped out of the dirigible, nearly tripping over his own feet, and raced to her. They sank to the ground and cried in each other's arms.

Several hours later, Cole found himself sitting at a table inside Arthur's laboratory. He was surrounded by Gabe, Arthur, Sabina, Brody, Ruby, and Karma.

"Now, Ruby, can you take us back to the beginning? How did this all start?" Arthur asked gently. Ruby was sitting at the table with a blanket draped around her and a stiff drink in her hand. She looked exhausted, but grateful to be alive. Her voice was soft and hoarse when she finally spoke.

"Well...it's difficult to remember everything. A lot of it is fuzzy because Jaxon kept me sedated most of the time."

"Just take your time and tell us whatever you can," Sabina said.

"What did he sedate you with?" Cole asked.

"He kept a pouch of this light pink powder with him at all times. I...I don't know what it was, but he blew it in my face and I would pass out."

"That sounds like Devil's Breath," Sabina said. "I helped write an article on it a few years ago. It's a powder that is derived from a South American shrub. It can render people unconscious."

Ruby took a deep breath and drank deeply from her cup. "I would lose hours of the day. Didn't know where I was half the time."

"I'm so sorry, Ruby," Brody said mournfully.

"Thanks Brody. It all started after our first date. Jaxon walked me to my apartment, and then everything suddenly went black. After that, he controlled everything about my life."

"But why did Jaxon target you? I don't understand," Cole said.

"I didn't understand for a long time, too. It didn't make sense. But then, one night, we were squatting in an abandoned building somewhere and this man showed up. The powder had worn off by then, but I stayed still and listened to their conversation. Jaxon laid out his entire plan."

"Who was the man?" Karma asked.

"I don't know. I'd never seen him before. The only thing that I remember is that he was very, very old. Oh, and he used a gold and silver wheelchair. I could only open my eyes a little bit, but it looked like it cost a fortune."

Arthur's face blanched and his expression darkened. He groaned in frustration.

"What is it, Arthur?" Karma asked.

"I...I actually know this man. His name is Gustav Fallowback. A nasty piece of work. He worked in the patent office. I was forced to fire him because he started harassing the mechanical staff and he would show up to work drunk. I never thought that I would ever hear about him again."

"Well, I overheard Jaxon mention that they met each other on an online anti-mechanical discussion board. Gustav told him to target me because of my connection to Dad. Jaxon is full of rage. He blamed you, and mechanicals, for everything: his father getting laid off, his suicide, as well as his mother's death. He hardly talked about anything else."

"Hmm...I wonder if his mother's death had anything to do with him suing the city for emotional distress," Sabina mused. "Did she die during the Malick Scandal?"

"Yes, I believe so," Ruby answered. "He accidentally killed her when he was possessed. Another reason why he hated mechanicals." She sagged in her seat from exhaustion, but she pressed on. "Anyway, that old man somehow knew about *The Astrolabe*."

"Impossible! No one at work knows about it!" Arthur cried.

"Did you ever leave a blueprint out at work? Could he have broken into your office?" Karma asked.

"I don't know...I guess it's possible, but..."

"I don't know how he found out, Dad, but he definitely brought it up to Jaxon. And then I...I..." Ruby put down her drink and sobbed loudly into her hands. "I told him how to find the entrance!"

"What?!" Cole cried.

"I didn't want to! Jaxon made me. You have to believe me, I would *never* tell anyone about *The Astrolabe!*"

"Of course we believe you, Ruby! It's not your fault." Cole reached over and grabbed her hand.

After a moment, Ruby regained her composure and drained her glass. "So...what now? Jaxon is dead, history has been restored, and all of the mechanicals are back. Gustav is still out there, though. What do we do about him?"

"Oh, we'll take care of him," Arthur said. "After we're done here, I'll be reaching out to Mayor Simpson. He'll be arrested by the end of the day."

The table that they were sitting at suddenly began to vibrate. A great rumbling sound rose in the air, and the various inventions standing in the laboratory toppled over onto the floor.

"What's happening?" Sabina cried.

"Not again!" Cole screamed.

The rumbling grew louder and louder until it was roaring in Cole's ears. He fell to the floor in pain. A blinding white flash filled the laboratory.

Moments later, everything fell still once again. The rumbling sound died down and the flash disappeared. Very slowly, Cole opened his eyes and looked around the room. He gasped and jumped to his feet; a tall figure that consisted of golden light was floating in the air in front of him. He couldn't tell if it was a man or a woman, and it was clear that the glowing being, looking down on everyone, wasn't human. An angry expression rested on their face and their arms were crossed.

"Well, you've really done it now. How *dare* you! You've made a *complete* mess of the Timeline!"

Humans First